MARIANNE DREAMS

Catherine Storr was born and lived most of her life in London. She practised medicine for fifteen years, but never forgot her ambition to be a writer. She wrote her first children's books for her three daughters and many went on to become classics. *Marianne Dreams* was made into a film, *The Paper House*, in 1990. She loved writing for children because they understand that fantasy and reality are not opposites – but different ways of looking at the same thing.

Marianne Dreams

CATHERINE STORR

ILLUSTRATED BY
MARJORIE-ANN WATTS

ff

faber and faber

First published in 1958
Reset and published in this paperback edition in 2000
by Faber and Faber Limited
Bloomsbury House
74–77 Great Russell Street
London WC1B 3DA

Photoset by Avon Dataset Ltd, Bidford on Avon
Printed in the UK by CPI Bookmarque, Croydon

A CIP record for this book is available from the British Library

ISBN 978–0–571–20212–6

6 8 10 9 7

Contents

1. Marianne's Birthday

Marianne had looked forward to her tenth birthday as being something special; quite different from any birthday she had yet had, for two reasons. First, that she was at last going into double figures, where she was likely to stay for a considerable time: and second, that her father and mother had promised that when she was ten she could have riding lessons, which was what she wanted more than anything else in the world. Marianne and her family lived, very unfortunately, she thought, in a town, and there was no question of keeping a pony, or riding at a farm, or competing at gymkhanas, like the lucky country children in the books which Marianne read. Even the milkman had given up the pony which used to pull his milk-cart when Marianne was a little girl, and now delivered milk from a boring sort of trolley that worked by electricity.

But there was a common near Marianne's home, and a riding stables the other side of the common, and on her birthday, the very day itself, fortunately a Saturday, she was to have her first lesson.

Marianne had imagined the lesson in a hundred different ways before it ever happened. Sometimes she rode a cream-coloured pony so beautifully that the riding master, or mistress, couldn't believe that she was a beginner and had never ridden before. Sometimes, forgetting her age and size, she rode a Shetland pony who, at first sight, loved and obeyed her, and was so unhappy when she left the stables that she had to be allowed to take it home and keep it. Sometimes, on her first visit to the stables, she met a nervous

[1]

Arab mare who appeared vicious and unsafe to her owners. Marianne had only to speak to her quietly, and lay a gentle hand on her black satin neck, and she became docile and tractable at once. The stable hands were amazed. 'We have never seen anything like this before,' they said. And so on, and so on, and so on.

Marianne knew that this was half nonsense and that people didn't become experienced horsewomen in an hour. And yet she half believed and hoped that something of the sort would happen and that her first riding lesson – especially as it was going to be actually on her birthday – would see her miraculously transformed into a finished rider, ready for the show ring.

Perhaps no riding lesson could have come up to quite so much expectation; the earlier part of the day exceeded all hopes with a totally unexpected wrist watch, a box of conjuring tricks, several new books, and a pair of riding gloves. Later in the morning Marianne realized that even a well-trained pony has a personality to be reckoned with, and that she had far more to learn about riding than she had ever dreamed of. But it was exciting to be on the back of a real horse at last; and the riding master, though he didn't say he couldn't believe she was a beginner, did say that she seemed to take to it naturally, which was as much as anyone in their senses could hope for.

It wasn't till the lesson was over, and she was home again, that Marianne realized how tired she was: not agreeably, after-exercise tired, but extraordinarily, aching tired all over; an unpleasant sensation. She dragged herself upstairs and changed out of her riding trousers, and then went down to the kitchen to find her mother and to see how her birthday lunch was getting on. It was when the smell of chicken and peas came floating up the kitchen stairs that she first realized that she wouldn't be able to eat any of it.

Not to be able to eat your lunch in the ordinary way is bad enough. It is worse if you have had your first riding lesson and know that you ought to be hungry. But not to be able to eat your birthday lunch is worst of all. A birthday lunch which you have chosen yourself is the peak of the day. You aren't, or shouldn't be, too tired to enjoy it, and there is still more to come. Marianne knew this. So when she saw the chicken, golden and crackling, and the roast potatoes and the peas and the bread sauce and the gravy, and found that as far as she was concerned they were all going to be wasted, she burst into tears.

'Darling, what's the matter?' her mother said, putting the hot plates down on the table very quickly and coming round to her.

'I don't know,' Marianne sobbed. She leant against her mother and tried to get comfort from her familiar smell. 'I can't eat any lunch.'

Her mother repressed some natural feelings of disappointment; after all, she had spent the best part of the morning cooking; and said, 'You're tired, darling. Perhaps the riding went on too long and you got too hot. I'll put it back in the oven and you can have it later.'

'I don't think I'll want it later,' Marianne said indistinctly, her face on her mother's shoulder.

'Never mind if you never want it, duckling, only stop crying. It won't waste, I can promise you, and I'll try not to let Thomas eat all the best bits. Come upstairs and cool down a bit – you're terribly hot.'

'I'm not,' said Marianne, surprised at her mother making such an obvious mistake. 'I'm cold. And my throat hurts. I think I must have swallowed a lot of dust while I was riding; at least, that's what it feels like – sort of gritty and aches a bit. And I'm terribly tired. I ache all over.'

So, instead of eating chicken and raspberries, Marianne went upstairs again. Her mother ran back into the kitchen to put on a kettle, and then came up to find the thermometer. And sure enough Marianne's temperature, when taken, was considerably higher than normal, and the only thing to do was to put her to bed and pile on blankets and give her the hot-water bottle for which the kettle had been put on to boil, and send for the doctor.

'I shall be well enough for my next riding lesson, shan't I?' asked Marianne, for perhaps the fourteenth time as her

mother moved about her bedroom, putting away her clothes, tidying up books and arranging all Marianne's birthday presents on the bookcase by her bed where she could see them easily.

'I hope so,' her mother said, also not for the first time. But she didn't sound very hopeful, and Marianne herself had by now reached a stage when she had ceased feeling very strongly about anything and she only continued to ask about her next riding lesson because that had been the last thing she felt as if she had really cared about. At the moment she was engrossed in feeling quite extraordinarily tired and yet not sleepy. Her throat ached and her head ached and her legs and arms felt hot and heavy and ached, too, and she didn't feel like riding at all. But even so she longed for her mother to say, yes, she would be able to have her next riding lesson, more than she longed for anything in the world, because that would be a promise that she would be better very quickly and wouldn't any longer feel so queer and unreal and not able to care about anything.

The doctor came later in the afternoon and said, as doctors so often do, that we must wait and see. He gave Marianne some medicine, which was soothing, and which made her aches better and her temperature drop a little. But he was quite emphatic that she was not to get up, even if she felt quite well the next day. He would come and see her again and then perhaps he'd be able to say what might be the matter.

But the next day he didn't say what it was, nor on the day after, and Marianne was sufficiently miserable not to care whether he could put a name to her illness or not. Everything seemed to have gone wrong, or rather different, as things tend to do when you are ill. It's like looking through the wrong end of a telescope and seeing things which you know are really quite close and which you could easily touch with your hand, looking tiny and far away. Marianne's birthday and the riding lesson and her school term, which had only just begun when she started to be ill, all receded into an immense distance. She knew they were there and had only just happened, but they had nothing to do with her. She didn't notice how the days passed. There was nothing to distinguish one from the other, and Marianne lost count. She felt as if she had never done anything else but lie in bed waiting. Sometimes she was waiting for the doctor, sometimes she was waiting for meals, in which she was strangely uninterested. Sometimes she was waiting for her mother to come back from shopping or her father to come home from work. A great deal of her waiting time she spent asleep or being read to by her mother and quite often falling asleep during the reading. But in a way she felt that it was still her tenth birthday. Because the illness had begun on her birthday itself, she had a feeling, especially as she gradually began to get better and to take more interest in what was going on, that when she was quite well and was up and about again, she would go on from exactly where she had left off: she even had a sort of feeling that if she went down to the kitchen she would find the table laid with her birthday lunch still waiting for her – roast chicken, bread sauce, raspberries and all.

2. The First Dream

Marianne had never been ill for more than a few days at a time; now she was horrified and fascinated to find the days becoming weeks, and the weeks adding up incredibly, so that it was almost a month before she felt like her real self enough to begin to worry about when she was to be allowed to get up. It was, in fact, exactly three weeks and two days after she had begun to be ill, when she sat up in bed waiting for her doctor to come and tell her that she could get up. She was feeling almost well again, and ready to amuse herself with something new; and it was on this day that she found the pencil.

It was in her great-grandmother's old polished mahogany workbox, which now belonged to Marianne's mother. It wasn't used as a regular everyday workbox for darning or mending or dressmaking, but was brought out occasionally for Marianne to look at and tidy up – generally when she was ill and tired of her own toys and books, and needing some extra amusement. The workbox was charming, and Marianne loved it. It had a tray lined with green satin and fitted with little tools with mother-of-pearl handles, for all sorts of elaborate, out-of-date, needlework; little satin-covered boxes with mother-of-pearl knobs on the lids, and a space underneath the tray, in which were all sorts of treasures that Marianne's great-grandmother and grandmother and mother had somehow collected. There were buttons of every kind, ivory lace bobbins, mother-of-pearl counters, an odd chessman or two, short lengths of ribbons, buckles, sequins, beads. Among them, this particular time, Marianne found the pencil.

She knew at once, as you do with some pencils, that it would be a nice one to use. It was stumpy, but long enough to hold comfortably; it had been sharpened with a knife, not a pencil sharpener, and Marianne could see that it would write clearly and blackly, without either scratching, or annoyingly breaking its point all the time. It was one of those pencils that are simply asking to be written or drawn with, and Marianne picked it out of the surrounding workbox muddle, seized her newish drawing book, and drew.

She drew, as she nearly always did, a house. A house with four windows and a front door. The walls were not quite straight, because she wasn't ruling the lines, and the chimney was a little large. Over the chimney she drew a faint scribble of smoke.

'It is a nice pencil,' Marianne thought. 'I'll ask Mother if I can keep it. She practically never uses anything out of the workbox, and I'm sure she wouldn't mind.'

She drew a fence round the house, and a path leading from the front door to a gate. She put some flowers inside the fence, and all around she drew long scribbly grass, which she hoped would be waist high at least. In the grass outside the fence she drew a few large rough-looking stones or lumps of rock, like those she had seen on the moors in Cornwall.

Marianne was no child prodigy at drawing. Like so many of us, she had often had ideas that if she had a particular set of coloured pencils, this tiny paintbox, or that very thick black pencil, she would suddenly find herself able to reproduce on paper the pictures she could see so clearly in her mind's eye. But somehow the magic never worked; and though this pencil had seemed to hold out the same sort of promise, her house looked as much like a shaky doll's house, and her grass as little like anything growing, as ever.

She was contemplating the result and feeling the usual pangs of disappointment at her own performance, when she heard her mother come up the stairs, talking to someone. Marianne knew it must be the doctor.

'Good,' she thought. 'Now he'll say I can get up and go back to school. I'm frightfully bored with being here all the time.'

But when the doctor had examined her, and asked all the usual sort of questions that doctors do ask, he didn't say she could get up and go back to school. In fact he still looked rather grave.

'Now, young lady,' he said, 'I don't know if this is going to be good news or bad news, but I'm afraid you won't be going back to school this term. You've got to stay in bed for at least another six weeks, possibly more. I'll come and see you fairly often and I'll tell you when you can get up, but until then, it's bed all the time.'

Marianne stared at him. She had never imagined anything like this. The three weeks she had already spent in bed had seemed endless and the idea of another six weeks, perhaps more, was terrible.

[9]

'But I must go back to school,' she protested. 'I'm acting in the school play at the end of term!'

'I'm sorry,' said Dr Burton. 'But you can't get up even for that.'

'But six weeks is a terribly long time,' said Marianne, 'I can't stay in bed for six weeks and not do anything.'

'I'm afraid you've got to,' Dr Burton said gravely. 'If you don't, you might make yourself ill in a way that would last the rest of your life, and we don't want that to happen.'

'I don't care,' Marianne said, nearly crying, 'I'd rather be ill for the rest of my life than have to stay in bed any more now.' She knew it was silly, and that she didn't really mean it, but she was too upset to mind.

'Well, I care,' said the doctor, 'I don't want to have to look after you as an invalid for another sixty years. I know it's upsetting and miserable, but it's got to be done. Now, cheer up. I'm going to come and see you very often, and your friends can come and visit you whenever you like; you're not infectious. You'll find it isn't anything like as bad as you expected. Good-bye.'

Although Marianne said good-bye in a rather choked voice, she didn't actually cry till Dr Burton had gone downstairs. But when she was sure he was out of earshot, she hid her face in the pillow and burst into tears. Her mother found her, a minute or two later, with a very red face and a very damp pillow.

'Poor love,' her mother said, sitting down on the side of the bed. 'I'm afraid you're very disappointed. But never mind, we'll think of all sorts of things to do, and the time will go very quickly, you'll see. I'm going to take out a subscription to the library especially for you, so you can have as many books as you want, and I'm arranging for someone, a sort of governess, to come and see you every day and give you a few lessons.'

'Mother!' Marianne said, so shocked that she quite stopped crying. 'Not *lessons*, when I'm ill!'

'Yes, darling, you'll enjoy reading to yourself and all the other things you do more if you don't do them all the time; and you'll find it's much easier when you go back to school if you've kept up a bit at home. Now, let me clear up your bed; it's rather a mess, isn't it? Did you tidy up my workbox? Was there anything interesting in it?'

'Yes, quite. I didn't finish,' Marianne said listlessly. She looked at the pencil lying on her bedside table, but without the interest she had felt before.

'I found that pencil,' she said, pointing. 'Can I have it, Mother? It's not silver or anything.'

'In my workbox? Yes, I should think so,' her mother replied. 'I don't remember seeing it before. Is that what you drew with it? It looks a nice house.'

'It isn't very,' Marianne said, rather crossly. 'I'm tired, Mother. I want to lie down.'

'Yes, do, my pet. Go to sleep till tea-time and you'll feel twice the woman. I've made jelly for tea.'

Marianne felt that no jelly could possibly comfort her, but she just managed not to say so. She lay down in a tight, uncomfortable ball, and wondered if she would sleep because she was so tired, or would lie awake and cry because she was so miserable; in fact, she was asleep before the door had shut.

Marianne dreamed.

She was in a great open stretch of country, flat like a prairie, covered, as far as she could see, with the long dry grass in which she was standing more than knee deep. There were no roads, no paths, no hills and no valleys. Only the prairie stretched before her on all sides till it met the grey encircling sky. Here and there it was dotted with great stones or rocks, which rose just above the level of the tall grass, like heads peering from all directions.

Marianne stood and looked. There seemed to be nothing to do and nowhere to go. Wherever she looked she saw nothing but grass and stones and sky, the same on every side of her. Yet something, a nagging uneasiness which she could not account for, drove her to start walking; and because at one point on the skyline she thought she could see something like a faint trickle of smoke, she walked towards that.

The ground under her feet was rutted and uneven, and the grass harsh and prickling. She could not move fast, and it seemed that she had walked a long way before she saw that she had been right about the faint line in the sky. It was a wavering stream of smoke, rising in the windless air from the chimney of a house.

It was a curious looking house, with leaning walls, its windows and door blank and shut. It rose unexpectedly straight from the prairie: a low uneven fence separated its small plot from the surrounding ground, though the coarse grass was the same within and without. There were some large pale yellow flowers about, which Marianne could not recognize, growing a foot or two high; they seemed to be as much outside the fence as in, and certainly did not constitute

a garden. Nothing moved except the thread of smoke rising from the chimney. In all that vast expanse nothing else moved.

There was a gate in the fence. Marianne pushed it open and walked up the path to the door. She did not much like the look of the house, with its blank staring windows and its bare front door, but she liked the prairie even less.

'I must get in,' said Marianne aloud in her dream. 'I've got to get in.'

There was no knocker and there was no bell. Marianne knocked with her knuckles, but it was a disappointing little noise and she was not surprised that no one answered. She looked around for a stone to beat on the door but the only stones were the great grey boulders outside the fence. As she stood, considering what to do, she heard the distant sound of wind. Across the prairie it blew towards her, and in its path the grass whistled and rustled, dry stalk on dry stalk, and bent, so that she could see the path of the wind as it approached her. Then it was all around her, and everything that had been so still before became alive with movement. The grass writhed and tore at its roots, the pale flowers beat against their stems, the thin thread of smoke was blown out like a candle flame, and disappeared into the dark sky. The wind whistled round the house and was gone, leaving Marianne deaf for a moment, and suddenly chilled.

'I'm frightened here,' she said. 'I've got to get away from the grass and the stones and the wind. I've got to get into the house.'

No voice spoke in reply to her words, and there was no signal from the silent house; but she knew the answer as if she had heard it.

'I could get in,' Marianne thought, 'if there was a person inside the house. There has got to be a person. I can't get in unless there is somebody there.'

'Why isn't there someone in the house?' she cried to the empty world around her.

'Put someone there,' the silent answer said.

'How can I?' Marianne protested. 'How can I put someone in the house? I can't get in myself! And I've got to get in!'

'I've got to get in!' she heard herself say, and the words woke her up. With difficulty she struggled back to realize that the house and prairie were gone: she was lying in bed, and the memory of the six weeks more to be spent there was lying in wait for her, to weigh down her spirits as soon as she was sufficiently awake to remember.

3. The Person in the House

For a day and a half Marianne was extremely unhappy. Not her mother's comforting, nor a brand-new and very ingenious bed-table ordered especially for her by her father, nor the knowledge that she was getting better, and would in time be quite well again, were enough to make her anything but miserable. She read, she ate, she played games with her mother, and she slept, in a haze of angry disappointment. It was only towards the end of the second day that she began to feel at all better about Dr Burton's decree. She had been asleep in the afternoon again – she seemed to spend a great deal of her time asleep – and she lay, after waking up, listening to the new leaves on the trees outside rustling in the wind. Those leaves had been only just bursting out of their buds when she had had her birthday; she wondered if they would be old yellow autumn leaves by the time she was quite well again. The whole summer, she felt, would have gone before she was allowed out of bed; and at the thought of the pleasures of the summer term, swimming baths, and hot, lazy games of rounders on grass, Marianne felt tears begin to prick her eyelids. But she didn't cry. The idea of staying in bed for so long did not now seem as preposterous, impossible and unreal as it had two days ago: it began to seem unescapable though unpleasant.

Marianne wondered what she would be like at the end of such a long time as an invalid. Would she be purified by suffering, like the heroines of old-fashioned books, who rose from their sick-beds changed – and always for the better? Or would she be just the same Marianne who had gone to bed on her birthday just over three weeks ago? She didn't see why staying in bed should alter her character very much, but yet she didn't feel exactly the same as she had even so short a time before. Somehow the feeling really ill had made a gap between the person she had been then, and the person she felt herself to be now, just as the six weeks which were to come, which were to keep her alone in bed, while everyone else went to school and played games and lived ordinary lives, seemed to separate her from the person she would have been if none of this had happened.

When she was sitting up in bed after tea, she looked, for the first time for two days, among the litter on her bedside table, with a renewed interest in doing something. She saw the pencil she had found in her great-grandmother's work-box, and again she felt that it was a pencil of character, a pencil which could draw if only she, Marianne, would let it. She picked it up and opened her drawing book, and saw the house she had drawn while she was waiting for the doctor; it seemed an age ago.

'But,' Marianne thought, suddenly interested, 'how extraordinary! It's the house in my dream!'

There were the blank windows: there was the rough grass and the great boulders around. There was the pencilled column of smoke, rising from the big chimney. There was the door without a knocker. Marianne's knuckles ached again as she remembered hammering on that bare front door.

It was the work of a moment to draw in a knocker, a front door handle and a letter-box on the door of her picture. She hesitated a moment before the next step.

'I said I didn't know how to put a person in the house to let me in,' she thought. 'But I can, of course. Now that I see I was dreaming about my own drawing.'

The windows were too small for her to draw a whole person looking out. She drew a head and shoulders at one of the upper windows; a boy's head, with short hair, because it was easiest to draw. It turned out to have rather a sad face, which Marianne hadn't meant, but she did not know how to alter it.

'There!' she thought, with satisfaction, as she finished. 'Now, if I dreamed about this place I would be able to get in, because the boy would come down and open the door. And I could knock properly with the knocker. I almost wish I would dream the same dream again, so that I could get inside and see what the house is like. But I don't suppose I shall. I wish there was a way of getting back into a dream that's been interesting.'

When her mother came up to begin getting her ready for the night, Marianne consulted her on the subject.

'Mother, can you make yourself dream something you want to?' she asked. 'I mean, if you've had a dream already that you liked having, could you get back into it again?'

'I heard of someone once who could go on in her dreams with stories she told,' her mother said. 'But I don't think I've ever actually known anyone who could choose what they were going to dream, if that's what you mean.'

'Bother!' Marianne said.

'Have you had a dream you want to get back into?' her mother asked.

'Yes,' was all that Marianne answered. She realized suddenly that she didn't want to be asked about the dream itself, and she changed the subject abruptly to governesses. All the time that her mother was clearing the room, washing her and brushing her hair, and while she ate her supper, she kept up a fire of questions about the governess her mother had engaged. Was she old? Very old? Was she strict? Would she have to be addressed as Ma'am? Would she insist on all conversation being in French? Marianne had never heard of a governess outside a Victorian children's book, and she pictured this specimen as an elderly lady with grey ringlets and possibly mittens and a cap, which for some reason made her mother laugh a great deal, though all she would say, in answer to Marianne's questions, was, 'wait and see'.

[17]

'I should think you'll dream about governesses tonight,' she said, when Marianne was fed and kissed and tucked up, and she was turning out the light.

'I don't want to,' Marianne said. 'Horrible people.'

'Good night, love,' her mother said.

'Good night, Mother darling.'

And again Marianne dreamed.

She was standing in long dry grass which rustled when she moved; behind and on both sides of her, as far as she could see, the same grass stretched, apparently for ever. In front of her, just the other side of a ragged, untidy fence, stood a house.

The house had leaning walls and a top-heavy chimney, from which a wisp of smoke rose straight into the grey windless sky. Marianne knew it at once.

'I've been here before,' she thought; but for a moment she could not remember when or where she had seen this house before. Yet it all seemed familiar – the long grass, the uneven fence, the path that led through the wild garden to the front door. Only the door itself looked somehow strange: and then, in an instant, Marianne remembered. She saw the knocker, the handle, and the letter-box, and she remembered how the last time she had been here she had bruised her knuckles on the door, trying to make someone inside the house hear. She remembered how the wind had blown cold fear all around her, and she felt again that the house was the only refuge she could find from something out here on the prairie which she did not understand. She remembered also that only another person could let her inside. She looked up at the windows on the first floor, and there, looking down at her from one of them, was the boy's face.

Marianne was startled. Then she waved. 'After all,' she thought, 'I've got to get into the house, so I may as well try to be friendly.'

The face changed, slowly. It smiled a little and a hand

[18]

waved back. It was rather a feeble wave, but it was not the gesture of an enemy.

Marianne pushed open the unlatched gate and walked into the garden with its pale yellow flowers. She went up to the front door, confidently put her hand on the knocker, and knocked loudly, ringingly. The inside of the house echoed to the noise as if it were a hollow shell.

But no one answered the door.

Marianne knocked again.

Still no one came.

Marianne stepped back and looked up at the right-hand window. The face was still there, and its owner had pressed it against the pane of glass so that the nose looked white and flat. The eyes were turned down in a squinting effort to see Marianne. She could now see the boy quite clearly. He had short, thick brown hair and freckles.

'Come down and let me in!' called Marianne. She didn't know how much he could hear through the closed window, and her voice sounded horribly loud.

The boy shook his head. He said something in reply, but

Marianne couldn't hear it. She shook her head in her turn.

'I can't hear you,' she shouted.

The boy began tugging at the window. It seemed very stiff, but at last he managed to move it. He got the lower sash up and put his head a little way out.

'You needn't shout,' he remarked, in a perfectly ordinary voice. 'In fact you'd better not. It isn't very safe round here.'

'Why?' asked Marianne. A little chill crept down her back and she looked quickly behind her. She saw only the fence, and beyond it the bare tussocky plain. Nothing stirred.

'Oh, well,' said the boy, and then he stopped. He didn't seem anxious to go on with the subject. Instead, he said, 'Why have you come here?'

'I don't know,' said Marianne. She thought, but she could not remember why or how she had come. 'I had to come,' she said, feeling as if this were true. 'I've got to get into this house.'

The boy seemed to understand this. He nodded.

'Why can't you let me in?' asked Marianne.

'I can't come down.'

'Why not?'

'Well, there aren't any stairs, to begin with.'

'No stairs! In the whole house? Then how did you get up there?'

The boy looked doubtful. 'I don't know,' he said. 'I was just here. And now I can't get down until there are stairs.'

'Can't someone else let me in?'

'There isn't anyone else,' said the boy. 'At least I don't think so. I haven't seen anyone except you.'

'Do you mean,' said Marianne, trying to be reasonable and friendly, though she felt extremely cross, 'that you live here, all by yourself, and you don't know how you got up there, when there aren't any stairs, or who looks after you, or where everybody else is, or anything?'

'Well, you don't really know how you got here, do you?' asked the boy. 'You don't know any more than I do.'

'I've got to get into the house,' said Marianne. It sounded stupid, but it was the only thing she felt sure of.

'And I've got to get out,' remarked the boy.

'You could almost jump,' said Marianne, measuring the height of the window from the ground. 'Perhaps I could catch you.'

'It'd probably break my legs and yours too if we tried,' said the boy disagreeably. 'Anyhow, you don't understand.'

'How can I understand when you don't explain anything?' Marianne cried out angrily. 'I was only trying to help. You can stay where you are then, I don't care. I don't want to have you jumping on top of me. Stay in your beastly house without any silly stairs and I hope nobody comes and you starve, that's all.'

She turned her back on the boy and the house and walked off down the path to the gate. The boy's voice followed her, faintly mocking. 'It's not my house, anyway, it's just as much yours. You've got to get in, remember?'

Marianne took no notice, except that she began to run, to get away the sooner. She ran through the gate and out into the field. Running was hard work; her legs wouldn't move quickly enough, her feet seemed to stick to the ground. Suddenly she caught her foot in one of the tussocks of grass and fell, with a shock that jolted her whole body.

She lay awake in bed.

4. Miss Chesterfield

Miss Chesterfield, who was the 'sort of governess' that Marianne's mother had engaged, came for the first time the next morning. She wasn't at all Marianne's idea of a governess, which was mostly taken from old-fashioned children's books. Instead of being middle-aged and rather prim and strict, she was quite young and very pretty. She was a little strict, perhaps, in not letting Marianne talk about other things while she was supposed to be doing sums and dictation, but when the two hours of lessons were over, she proved to be very friendly and quite prepared to listen to Marianne and to talk herself. Marianne, who had never met a real live governess before, wanted to know a lot about her: what it was like being a governess, how she had started to be one, whom else she had taught, and what the other children were like. Apparently Miss Chesterfield had never lived with one family for years and years, watching them all grow up from the nursery to the schoolroom and the schoolroom to the grown-up world, as Marianne had imagined – though Miss Chesterfield looked as if she hadn't been grown up herself for very long. Instead of this, she went round from one family to another, teaching children who for some reason or other couldn't go to school for a time. She had taught a blind boy called Robert, and a family of six little girls who were in quarantine for chicken-pox, and all got it, one after the other. She had gone on a sailing holiday one summer with a mother and father and three children who were terribly bad at arithmetic and all had to be taught from the very beginnings. She also had one or two regular pupils

[22]

whom she went to once or twice every week for special subjects. One of these, it appeared, was a girl of thirteen, called Evelyn, who was learning Latin and French and was rather clever. Another one was a boy called Mark, who was recovering very slowly from a bad illness which had left him partly paralysed. He hadn't been at school for six months and Miss Chesterfield was keeping him more or less up to standard in all the important subjects, such as Latin and mathematics and French, so that he wouldn't be too much behind the others when he went back.

'Will he get better?' Marianne asked. 'I mean will he be able to walk again?'

'Yes, the doctors think he probably will,' Miss Chesterfield said. 'But it depends very much on what he does in the next month or two. If he really tries, they think he could recover completely perhaps, but of course if he doesn't try he probably won't.'

'But how can he not try?' Marianne exclaimed, astonished. 'Doesn't he want to get well? He can't want to stay in bed for the rest of his life.'

'I don't think he'd say he wanted that,' Miss Chesterfield agreed. 'But in some ways Mark is lazy. Of course he's been ill for a long time now and it's very difficult for him to get back to ordinary life. He's a clever boy, too, and he's always read a great deal, and it would be very easy for him now just to be content to be an invalid, or partly an invalid for a long time – I really don't think he'd mind terribly as long as he could get enough books to read.'

'How extraordinary,' Marianne said, 'I don't feel as if I'd ever get used to staying in bed, and I do quite like reading. But if Dr Burton said tomorrow that I could get up, I would. Straight away.'

'I think Mark would if it was just a question of getting up,' Miss Chesterfield said. 'But you see it isn't for him. He's been in bed so long that his muscles have to be trained all over again to do their work properly. He'll have to learn to walk again, and it's tiresome and it hurts sometimes, and it all seems more bother than it's worth when he doesn't feel very well anyhow.'

'We're just the opposites, him and me, aren't we?' Marianne said thoughtfully. 'He's got to take exercise and doesn't want to, and I've got to stay in bed and I don't want to do that. It's a pity you can't mix us up a bit, Miss Chesterfield, so that I could do his energetic things for a bit and he could lie in bed and read for me.'

'I dare say you're each of you better off as you are,' Miss Chesterfield said. 'And now stop exercising your tongue, Marianne, and concentrate on your work. You've got to find out how long it takes to fill a sixty-gallon cylinder with a pump which produces a quarter of a pint every ten seconds, and it's a perfectly possible sum so don't make that face.'

Marianne did the sum – and got it wrong, but that was because she made a mistake in multiplication and not because she didn't understand the principle of the problem, which was what Miss Chesterfield said was most important. But she did make the face, which meant that it was really very difficult, several times, and she also continued to think about Mark, which perhaps accounted for her making the mistake. But although she tried in every possible way to get Miss Chesterfield to talk about Mark, or indeed about any of her other pupils during lesson time, she wasn't successful. Miss Chesterfield insisted on keeping very seriously to the time-table she had made out for Marianne and herself, and mathematics was followed by history, and history by French, and then it was the end of the morning's work, and Miss Chesterfield had to go.

'But you'll tell me all about Mark and Robert and the chicken-pox little girls tomorrow, won't you?' Marianne urged her, as she put away the books they had been using and tidied up Marianne's bed.

'Tomorrow,' said Miss Chesterfield, pretending to look very stern, 'I shall probably set you to learn all the dates of all the Kings and Queens of England, and the tables of weights and measures. We shan't have time for any idle gossip.'

'Not idle gossip, exactly,' Marianne protested, 'just tell me a little about Mark. Tell me if he's good at sums and history and things. Is he better than I am at seeing how to do problems, Miss Chesterfield? Or doesn't he have to do things like that if he's paralysed and can't walk?'

'Certainly he has to,' said Miss Chesterfield briskly. 'And history, and French and Latin as well. And now I must go, Marianne, and you must stop asking questions. Tomorrow we'll have lessons first and questions afterwards, if there's time for them. Otherwise I see we shall never get any work done at all, and you'll go back to school next term knowing as much as I do about my other pupils and nothing about anything else.'

Marianne found she got used surprisingly quickly to having lessons every morning; and her mother had been right about it making the rest of the day seem more interesting. She liked the lessons too, most of them, and she liked Miss Chesterfield, and on the whole staying in bed wasn't as bad as she had expected. But there were times when she thought of what she was missing, about the school play and the parties she couldn't go to, and the swimming baths and dancing and the cheerful noise of the cloakroom at school at the end of the day when everyone was dressing to go home and shouting at the top of her voice to make her friends hear the latest news. When she thought about these things Marianne was very sad. Sometimes she cried, at first, secretly into her pillow so as not to let anyone know. Later other things got unbearable, such as not being allowed to fetch her own books and toys when she wanted to, nor being able to go and see who had come to the door when visitors arrived, having to wear the same pyjamas – not the same pair, of course, but the same kind of garment – all the time, and other small but annoying restrictions. She got used to being in bed and seemed almost to forget what it was like to be well and allowed to get up and run about; and yet she was bored. Sometimes she was so bored that she couldn't think of a single thing she could bear to do. She didn't want to read a new book or do a puzzle or write a letter or knit or sew or even see a new face. She only wanted to be left to be miserable. But fortunately she didn't very often feel like this; and when she did, things always improved when Miss Chesterfield came to give her lessons or when her mother was free to read to her or to play games with her. Then, except for being tired of bed, Marianne felt better again, and the time, instead of standing still, started moving again at a reasonable pace, so that the mornings went quickly by and the afternoons and evenings not much slower than afternoons do for well and up-and-about people.

Miss Chesterfield kept quite strictly to the rule of lessons first and questions afterwards, but in spite of this Marianne found out quite a lot about Robert and Mark and the six little girls, who had all been given names beginning with the letter F. This was not so bad, though perhaps muddling, for Frances, Felicity, Faith and Fiona. But Marianne and Miss Chesterfield agreed that it was hard on Fenella and Ferelith to have quite such unusual names just to fit in with an idea of their parents, which really wasn't such a good one in the first place. Their surname was Frammington, which made it all the worse.

It was on the day when she'd been hearing about the six little chicken-pox girls that Marianne dreamed again. Ordinarily she didn't sleep in the daytime, but there had been a thunderstorm the night before which had kept her awake, and in the afternoon, after Miss Chesterfield had gone, she was sleepy. She had been drawing again: she wasn't quite pleased with the house she had drawn before. She found, which was a nuisance, that she couldn't rub out the marks made by the pencil, although it didn't look like an indelible one: so all she could do was to add to the picture she had drawn already. She drew a background – a line of hills, dipping and curving into each other like the South Downs, and a narrow road leading up to the top of the hills from somewhere out of the picture.

The garden round the house looked a little empty, so she put in a little apple tree, which came out rather crooked because there wasn't quite room for it between the fence and the house.

'On the other side of the hills,' said Marianne to herself, 'is the sea.'

She looked at the face she had drawn at the window and remembered how she had dreamed about a boy in this house and how he had said there were no stairs, so he couldn't come down to open the door. On the opposite page in her drawing-book she drew a flight of stairs. They didn't look at all convincing. Marianne knew there was a special way of drawing stairs which made them look real, but she couldn't remember it. To show that her stairs really were stairs, she began to draw the inside of the house round them. She drew a hall downstairs in which the stairs began, and two rooms leading off it, one on either side. She drew it all flat, as if you were looking into an opened doll's house. The stairs now quite clearly led up to the first-floor landing, where Marianne drew some banisters and a small clock. Two more rooms led out of this landing, and in one of these she put a very small figure – a sort of pin man, there wasn't room for more – for the boy.

It was at this point that she became too sleepy to be able to keep her eyes open any longer. She lay back in bed and was asleep, with the pencil still in her hand.

5. Inside

Marianne dreamed.

She was in a room: it was a big bare room, with no furniture in it at all. She was standing in the middle of the room, half-way between the window, which was rather high up, and the door.

There didn't seem any point in standing still in an empty room, so Marianne went to the window. By standing on tiptoe she could just see out. There was long grass outside, growing from as far as she could see right up to the window, though a little distance away there was a fence. It was not a very interesting view and Marianne turned her back on it and went towards the door. Her shoes sounded horribly loud on the stone floor. They echoed. Even a wooden floor in an unfurnished, uncarpeted room will make a very loud noise when walked on, but the stone floor made much more. It was a little frightening. Marianne wondered whose house she was in and whether anyone would hear her moving about. When she thought of this she walked on tiptoe, but she still couldn't be completely silent.

She opened the door: it opened easily. Outside was a large square hall, also unfurnished. A flight of wide, shallow, stone steps led up from the hall to a landing above. On the opposite side of the hall, facing Marianne, was another door.

The house was very quiet. If anyone had heard Marianne clattering on the stone floor, they had not taken any notice. But there was not the absolute silence of a deserted house. Marianne, as she came through the door, had felt certain, without knowing why, that the house was lived in. There was something going on, something which at first she couldn't put a name to, something that went with houses inhabited by families, that went with ordinary life, that went with people; and it was in this house. It might have been a smell – because, although we very seldom realize it, we respond to smells a great deal more than we know; and the smell of an empty house is quite different from the smell of one that is lived in. This house had no smell, and this alone would have been extraordinary. It felt like those imitation houses which are put up for show or advertisement, in exhibitions or on the stage. Those houses have no smell: you could tell with your eyes shut and your hands tied behind you that they are not real and not only are not lived in, but never have been and never will be lived in. There is, or used to be, in London, a row of houses which backed on to a railway, and one of the houses, in the angle where the road meets the rail-track, is a sham and has no thickness at all, although in front it has a door and windows and is got up to look like an ordinary house to match the others in the row. That house, if it existed, would have the same no-smell. It's a curious sort of flatness which tells you of something not being there.

But it wasn't the no-smell that Marianne noticed. Something else was contradicting the smell-lessness of the house and the lack of furniture, the emptiness of the room and hall and the echoing sound of her footsteps. The something else was a sound, the regular ordinary tick of a clock.

It had been ticking all the time, of course, saying in its matter-of-fact and comforting way that this house wasn't completely unreal. Anyone who has a clock with a loud and reassuring tick, and who bothers to keep the clock wound, must be somewhere about and probably worth finding. That was what Marianne felt, with relief. She hadn't been actually frightened – in fact, at first, finding herself in an apparently empty house, she had been pleased that at any rate there seemed to be no one to be cross with her for being there.

Now she felt even more pleased that there was somebody here, and she decided to go and find them.

The tick came from upstairs, so she went up. The clock stood, she found, on a little shelf just at the head of the flight, on a landing. Below the clock was a door, and because it was under the clock, Marianne decided to try this room first. She knocked.

A voice said, 'Come in.'

Marianne opened the door and walked in.

This room was unfurnished too, but not unoccupied. Sitting on a low window seat and looking towards her was a boy, and directly she saw him, Marianne knew him. Last time she had seen him she had been outside the house and she hadn't seen more than his face and hands, but there was no doubt that he was the same boy. He was longer than she had expected, and perhaps a little older, but still pale and freckled and brown-haired.

'So you got in after all,' the boy said.

Marianne's mind did a sort of prodigious leap. It jumped from uncertain ground in the dark to sure-footed certainty. In this moment Marianne understood that she was now inside the house she had before only seen from the outside; that she had got where she felt she must get to and that she was talking to the boy whom she had left before in more or less of a temper. He didn't seem to be annoyed now, any more than he had been before; only perhaps a little teasing. He hadn't appeared surprised to see her. He'd spoken almost as if he'd expected her to come, and as if they had only just stopped talking to each other, with her outside in the garden and him inside in the house.

'I got in,' Marianne repeated. She was still standing only just inside the door, feeling bewildered by so much going through her mind all at once. She knew she had spoken slowly and rather stupidly, and she wasn't surprised at the boy saying sharply, 'Yes, you got in. Now wake up and tell me how you did it?'

'Did what?' Marianne asked, still slowly.

'Got in, silly. How did you get in? I didn't let you in, so who –? I mean, did anyone else let you in?'

'No,' Marianne said. 'There isn't anyone else.' She wondered as she said it, how she was so sure of this.

'That's what I thought.' The boy leant back against the embrasure of the window seat as if he were relieved about something.

'But there are stairs,' Marianne said. She shut the door behind her and came over to the window. The boy, now she saw him close to, looked tired and unwell. He was very pale, in spite of the freckles, and there were dark shadows under his eyes. He looked as if he hadn't gone out into the sunshine or slept properly for a long time. Marianne sat down on the other end of the window seat and looked at him. 'There are stairs,' she said again, as he didn't answer.

'Oh, are there?' the boy said indifferently.

'But you said there weren't any.'

'There weren't when I said so. They must have come since.'

'But how could they come?' cried Marianne in exasperation. 'When the house was built already and you were upstairs? How could you be up here and the stairs come afterwards? It's nonsense! They must have been here all the time when you said you couldn't come down because there weren't any stairs.'

'Keep your hair on,' said the boy disagreeably.

'And anyway,' said Marianne, 'they're old stairs. They're not new, they're old. You can see where people have walked on them and worn the steps down, and the banister is all smooth where people's hands have gone. Come and see if you don't believe me.'

She jumped up and went towards the door. But the boy made no attempt to follow her and she stopped, half-way.

'Aren't you coming?' she asked.

'No. I believe you. There's a complete flight of stairs outside, with old steps and a shiny handrail, and it looks as if thousands of people had been up and down it thousands of times. All right. But it wasn't there yesterday.'

'Yesterday?'

'Nor the other day when you were here. Outside, I mean, saying you'd got to get in.'

'But how could it –?'

'I don't know. I don't know how lots of things round here work. The stairs are only one of the things that suddenly came. For instance, look out of the window.'

Marianne looked. It was the same view that she had seen from the window below, but now she could remember how she had walked over that long tussocky grass on the endless field outside the garden fence. The garden had the same sort of grass in it, not a proper lawn, and among the long grass grew the same pale flowers she had seen before.

'Look down and a bit to the side,' said the boy.

Marianne peered downwards and sideways. There was

nothing very startling or even interesting to be seen. Close to the side wall of the house was a little stunted apple tree with some apples on it. They didn't look ripe, but yet they also didn't look exactly unripe, and Marianne wondered for a moment if they were real. They looked almost like artificial fruit which never goes bad but also never ripens and can never be eaten.

'Do you see that tree?' asked the boy.

'Yes. There's nothing very special about it, is there?'

'Only that it wasn't there just now.'

'What do you mean, wasn't there?'

'Just what I say. It wasn't there. There was just grass and those flowers. And then next time I looked, there was the tree.'

'Had someone come and planted it?' Marianne asked.

'No, I'd been sitting here all the time and never heard a sound. And anyhow there wasn't time. It just appeared.'

'How long have you been here?' Marianne asked. She wasn't sure how much she believed the story about the tree, but she was definitely interested in the boy himself.

'I don't know,' he answered shortly.

'Well, about?'

'I don't know, I tell you.' He sounded angry.

'Is it a long time?' Marianne persisted. 'I mean is it weeks or days?'

'I haven't counted,' he said.

'But you can't live here,' said Marianne, struck by a new idea. 'There isn't any furniture. Or are the other rooms properly furnished? You can't go to bed here. What do you do at night?'

'You ask an awful lot of questions,' the boy said, scowling.

'Well, you're so mysterious. I don't believe you know anything more than I do about this place. I believe you've only just come here and you're pretending to be very wise and clever and making me seem stupid and inquisitive and really you don't know anything at all.'

She stopped.

'Temper,' said the boy.

'Well, what do you know?'

'You're right in a way,' the boy admitted. He turned his face away from her and looked out of the window. 'I don't know much about this place.'

'What do you know?'

'Well, I don't know where we are, and I don't know how we got here. Look, if you'll calm down a bit, and sit down again instead of standing in the middle of the floor and stamping, I'll tell you.'

Marianne came over to the window seat and sat down. She tucked her legs underneath her comfortably, and said, 'Well, go on then.'

The boy seemed to hesitate. He looked round the empty room – empty except for themselves – and out of the window.

'I don't know much more than you do,' he repeated, at last. 'I just found myself here. In this room. Like you found yourself out there, didn't you?'

Marianne nodded.

'I didn't know what the place was like. I mean, I could look out of the window, in fact that was the first thing I found myself doing; but I didn't know, still don't, what the outside of this house is like. All I could see was the grass and the daisies, or whatever those flowers are, outside. And you. And you said you'd got to find your way in.' He stopped.

'Well?'

'Well, I thought that was funny because I'd got the same sort of feeling, only different.'

'But you were in,' said Marianne.

'Yes, but I felt – well, anyway, that doesn't matter. Then you ran away and I don't remember any more. Of that time, at least.'

'How d'you mean, of that time?'

'I'm not here all the time,' the boy explained. 'Sometimes I find I'm here, sometimes I'm not. When I am here I sit on this window-sill most of the time. But I've never spent a whole night here.'

'How often have you been here?'

'I don't know. Five or six times, I think. Whenever I get back I sort of know I've been here before, and I seem to know something about it, but I never know when I'm coming.'

'No, I don't either,' Marianne said. 'But I still don't understand about the stairs.'

'What about them?'

'You said there weren't any.'

'There weren't, either.'

'How do you know?'

'I did know when you asked me,' the boy said, slowly. He sounded slightly puzzled. 'But I'm not sure how I knew. Afterwards I went and looked and there weren't any – in fact there wasn't anything. It was rather beastly.'

'How do you mean, there wasn't anything?'

'No stairs, nothing. Just empty.'

'But there's a clock, and a hall downstairs and other rooms. How could there be nothing?'

The boy shook his head.

'I don't know. But there wasn't. It was dark and I didn't like it.'

'But I still don't understand how you knew about the stairs,' Marianne persisted. 'Before you looked, I mean.'

'I don't know quite how I knew,' the boy said. 'It's something to do with being here. It's like your knowing you'd got to get into this house.'

'Oh, yes, and you said something about that, too. Wait a moment,' said Marianne, though the boy hadn't spoken, 'I'll remember in a minute. You said you'd felt something too, but you didn't say what. You said it was the same as my feeling only different.'

[36]

'Yes,' said the boy, but he said nothing else.

'Well?' said Marianne impatiently.

'Well what?'

'Your feeling. What was it? I don't see how you could feel you'd got to get in when you were already. What did you feel?'

'It's silly,' said the boy, wriggling a little on the window seat, as if he was embarrassed.

'Never mind,' said Marianne encouragingly. 'Perhaps my feeling was silly, but I did tell you and I did get in.'

'I don't suppose it's anything, really,' the boy said.

'But you do feel something,' Marianne urged.

'I just feel as if I'd got to get out. Mind you, it's being cooped up here, I expect, and getting tired of one room and a bit bored with having nothing to do except look out of the window. It's just an ordinary sort of feeling anyone might have who'd been in the same room for a long time.'

'Why don't you go out?' asked Marianne reasonably.

'Well, I couldn't when there weren't any stairs,' the boy answered quickly.

'Yes, but now? The stairs are there now and you could just walk down them.'

'I can't,' said the boy. He flushed.

'You can't?'

'I can't walk.'

'But I don't understand,' Marianne cried out in exasperation. 'What on earth is the matter? First of all you say you can't go down to let me in at the door because there aren't any stairs, and now you say you can't walk, so you can't use them now the stairs are there!'

'Shut up!' said the boy.

'And anyhow,' said Marianne, far too much excited to shut up at this point. 'If you can't walk, how do you know there weren't any stairs before? You said you went and looked. How could you, if you can't walk?'

The boy flushed more than ever.

[37]

'I did look. I got to the door and opened it and I looked.'

'How?' jeered Marianne. 'If you really can't walk, how did you get to the door? I suppose you crawled there?' She was scornful.

The boy didn't answer. His head was turned away and he was apparently looking out at the garden. Marianne looked down, for the first time, at his legs. They were thin, terribly thin, not at all like the stout, well-muscled, grey-stockinged legs of her young brother, Thomas. These legs looked as if they had not been used for a long time – might perhaps never be used again.

'Have you been ill?' she asked at last, gently.

The boy nodded, but didn't speak. Nor did he turn his head.

'I'm sorry,' Marianne said. 'I didn't know.'

'It's all right,' the boy said.

'I'm afraid I was beastly,' Marianne said apologetically.

'It's all right,' the boy repeated. He looked round at Marianne and gave her a half-smile.

'Were you always – I mean, could you walk all right before you were ill?' Marianne asked, emboldened by the smile.

'Yes, of course. It's only this foul disease that made my legs go wrong, and my back. I was perfectly all right before.'

'Isn't it just weakness after being ill?' Marianne suggested.

The boy shook his head.

'It's the disease itself,' he said. 'It does something to your muscles and then they don't work properly. I got over the feeling ill part of the thing ages ago – months. But I still can't walk properly, or hold myself up like I used to.'

'But you will,' Marianne cried.

'They don't know. No one knows. They say if I practise, probably, perhaps. But no one can be sure. And I hate the exercises, they're boring and I get tired and they don't seem to do any good.'

Marianne, suddenly struck by inspiration at the word exercises, said,

'You're Mark. I can't remember your other name – Miss Chesterfield never uses it. But you are Mark, aren't you?'

'Yes,' said the boy. He looked surprised. 'I'm Mark. Who are you?'

Marianne opened her mouth to answer, but as she did so the clock on the landing outside began to strike, and the sound, growing mysteriously louder and louder, drowned her voice saying her own name. She could see from Mark's face that he couldn't hear her. She leant forward, she raised her voice, she shouted. And still the clock struck. She made a tremendous effort, stretching her mouth and cracking her lungs in an effort to make herself heard.

And woke.

6. The Row

Before she had been ill Marianne had seemed to herself (and, it is fair to say, to most other people) to be a good-tempered child. That is not to say that she never got angry, or smacked Thomas, her young brother, when he annoyed her: but on the whole she very seldom really lost her temper, and on the rare occasions when she did, she had recovered again very quickly.

But now she had had to stay in bed for so long, Marianne found it increasingly difficult to feel or to be agreeable. A great many things seemed to annoy her which she had never noticed as being at all annoying before, but which had now become unbearably irritating. She hated people being later than they had promised in coming to see her, or stopping downstairs, after they had arrived, talking to the rest of the family before coming up: she hated having to wait for the things she wanted which were out of reach and had to be brought to her. She hated hot sunny days when her bed got warm and sticky and there wasn't a cool place to lie on or a comfortable position to get into, and flies buzzed in and out of the window and round and round the electric-light bulb ungetatably. She hated waking in the middle of the night and not being able to go to sleep again, a thing which had never happened to her before, but quite often occurred now she couldn't go out or take any sort of exercise to make her comfortably tired. And she hated also the bored sort of tiredness which she seemed to have for such a lot of the time – not good, after-exercise, sleepy, healthy tiredness which is cured by a hot bath and a long night's sleep in bed, but the

unpleasant tiredness which is known and dreaded by anyone who has had to stay in bed for any length of time. It was
this feeling that made Marianne wonder sometimes if she
had suddenly become a bad-tempered sort of person or
whether she had really always been like this but it hadn't
shown before. It seemed to need an effort, quite a lot of the
time, to behave with quite ordinary politeness, and it was
an effort she had never before needed to make.

And then one day she just couldn't make the effort any
longer, and the storm broke.

It was a day that had begun with high hopes, which made
it all the worse. Marianne had discovered, about a week
earlier, that this day was Miss Chesterfield's birthday, and
she was going to give her a present. After a good deal of
discussion, and changing her mind several times, she had
made up her mind that what Miss Chesterfield would like
best would be roses: so she had commissioned her father,
who passed a wonderful flower-shop on his way to and
from work every day, to buy as many as he could for two
shillings and fourpence, which was all the money she could
raise at the time. And the evening before, Marianne's father
had brought home nine perfect roses – and a penny change
– four dark red and five golden yellow, and they were in a
jug of water in Marianne's bedroom, hidden behind her bed
so that at the right moment she could bring them out and
present them to Miss Chesterfield.

She had also done some rather difficult problems in
mathematics which Miss Chesterfield had set her the day
before, and she had a feeling that she had done them right,
which was satisfactory. But it made her all the more anxious
for Miss Chesterfield to appear, and before half past nine,
which was her usual time for arriving, Marianne was listening to every footstep on the pavement outside the house,
wondering if this one was Miss Chesterfield; or this, or this,
or this or this.

But for almost the first time since she had started coming

to teach Marianne, Miss Chesterfield was late.

At about a quarter to ten the telephone bell rang. Marianne hardly noticed it. She was still listening for the sound of footsteps coming up to the front door, but a moment later her mother came to the door of her room.

'Marianne, that was Miss Chesterfield on the telephone. She's very sorry she's late, but she was asked especially to go round to one of her other pupils on the way here, and she got held up there. She was just ringing up to say she would be here in ten minutes and to apologize for keeping us waiting.'

Marianne didn't reply.

'Didn't you hear, Marianne?' her mother asked. 'Miss Chesterfield has got delayed and –'

'I heard the first time,' Marianne interrupted crossly. 'Why should she go somewhere else on the way here? She's supposed to be here at half past nine and it's nearly ten o'clock. She hasn't any right to do that.'

'I suppose if these other people asked her to go in on her way here, she thought it wouldn't matter very much to us,' Marianne's mother said reasonably. 'After all, if she starts half an hour later here, she can go on half an hour extra at the end of the morning. It doesn't make any difference to you.'

'It does,' Marianne said indignantly. 'I hate being kept waiting any morning, but it's especially annoying this morning because of the flowers and it being her birthday.'

'But she couldn't know you are going to give her anything,' Marianne's mother argued. 'And anyhow she obviously didn't think she'd be kept so long, or she'd have rung up before she started, to say she'd be late. I'm sorry you've had all this waiting, darling, but don't be cross when she does come. After all, it is her birthday, and you've got a very nice present for her and I'm sure she'll be awfully pleased.'

Marianne looked down at the jug of roses by her bed and felt more cheerful.

'I wish I'd been able to get more of them, though,' she said, in quite an ordinary voice again. 'It's a pity they're sold in such an expensive way – separately, I mean, not for so much a bunch. Still, they are beautiful, aren't they, Mother? I do hope Miss Chesterfield won't mind there being only nine, but you can see they are specially good ones, can't you? So she wouldn't expect a whole big bunch, would she?'

'No,' her mother began, but then the front door-bell rang, and she said, 'I expect that is Miss Chesterfield now. Bridget will let her in and I must go out. I've got to go into town and I shan't be back till this afternoon. Have a nice morning, my poppet, and I hope all your sums are right and that Miss Chesterfield loves the roses.'

She disappeared. Marianne could hear the sounds of Miss Chesterfield being let in downstairs, and after a moment or two she heard her coming up. She had planned in her own mind what she was going to say, 'Many happy returns of the day,' the moment Miss Chesterfield opened her door, but her door was already open and Miss Chesterfield was speaking before she could say anything.

'I am so sorry I'm late, Marianne. I know how annoying it is to be kept waiting, and that's why I telephoned. Mrs Grantham, Mark's mother, rang me up very early this morning and wanted me to call in on my way here, as she knew I practically pass the door, and then it took longer than I expected.'

'What did?' Marianne asked suspiciously.

She was inclined to be a little jealous of Mark in any case, in spite of her interest in him, and she felt sore and angry now that Mark should have had Miss Chesterfield first on this special morning when she had so much wanted her.

'It was Mark's idea,' Miss Chesterfield said. She sounded embarrassed and pleased. 'He knew it was my birthday, and as this isn't one of the days I go there in the ordinary way, he wanted me to go in extra for just a moment so that he could give me – wait, I'll show you.'

She ran out of the room and down the stairs, leaving Marianne curious, exasperated and anxious. She hated being left like this – why, oh why, couldn't she just run after her and say, 'I'll come and look myself,' as she would have been able to a month or so ago? And she had a horrid feeling that she knew what Mark had given Miss Chesterfield and she didn't want to see it. Yet it was even worse than she'd feared. Miss Chesterfield came in smiling, a little out of breath from her run upstairs, holding out in front of her for Marianne to admire, a really enormous bunch of roses. And they were beautiful roses too, quite as good as Marianne's and about six times as many.

'There,' said Miss Chesterfield, 'aren't they lovely? My favourite flowers, and such beauties! Look, I'll give you some, Marianne. Would you like one of each colour?' She started gathering them together as she spoke.

There was a silence.

'You'd like them, wouldn't you?' Miss Chesterfield repeated, surprised at getting no answer. 'I'm sure Mark wouldn't mind and I can easily spare you some out of such a big bunch.'

'No,' said Marianne.

'Oh, yes,' said Miss Chesterfield cheerfully, misunderstanding Marianne's answer. 'I'll have quite enough left, really. Look, I'll put yours beside you here, on this table, and then you can arrange them as you like.'

Marianne didn't answer. She looked at the roses, sourly. She knew she ought to be grateful and to sound pleased, but it was more than she could do. It was only by not speaking and swallowing hard that she was preventing herself from bursting into tears of rage and disappointment.

'What's the matter, Marianne?' Miss Chesterfield asked anxiously. 'Don't you feel well?'

Marianne found it easiest to shake her head and bury her face in the pillow. 'I'll go and call your mother,' Miss

Chesterfield said, and went quickly out of the room.

When she had gone, Marianne sat up. She was angry, so angry that she felt she must do something violent to express her feelings. She threw all the roses, Mark's roses, which Miss Chesterfield had given her, on the floor, where they lay in a sad wet heap; but somehow that did not express any feelings as fierce as Marianne felt hers to be. She longed to smash something, to kick or bite or scratch, to hurt something terribly to show just how much she had been hurt.

She looked all round. There wasn't much within reach – only the nine roses she had bought herself to give Miss Chesterfield. She had a quite unreasonable feeling that she wouldn't throw them about because that was how she had treated Mark's roses, and she wouldn't give them the same treatment as his had received. On the table by her bed was a small pile of books – mostly school books and exercise books which she used in her lessons. It seemed silly to do anything to them. Even though she was in a temper she could recognize that hurting them wouldn't make her feel any better.

Then her eyes fell on her drawing book. She snatched it up. It opened at her page of the drawing of the house, with the boy, who had been Mark in her dream, looking out. Marianne picked up the pencil, which had been lying beside the book and scored thick lines across and across and up and down over the window.

'I hate Mark,' she was saying to herself, under her breath. 'I hate him, I hate him, I hate him. He's a beast, and he's spoiled my present. I hate him more than anyone else in the world and I wish he was dead.'

She scribbled viciously over the face in her picture, and felt as if it really was Mark she was destroying. The house had begun to look like a prison now, with thick crossed lines like bars over the window, and Marianne took an evil pleasure in heightening the resemblance. She made the fence round the sad little garden thicker and higher, so that it enclosed the house like a wall round a prison. Outside it were the great stones and boulders she had drawn before, reminding her of gaolers. They should watch Mark, she thought with angry satisfaction, keeping him prisoner under constant surveillance. Marianne drew in more stones, a ring of them round outside the fence. To each she gave a single eye.

'If he tried to get out of the house now, they would see,' Marianne thought. 'They watch him all the time, everything he does. They will never let him out.'

She was so much engrossed that she had actually forgotten that Miss Chesterfield had gone to fetch her mother, until she saw her come back again and stand, hesitating, at the door.

'How do you feel?' she asked, seeing Marianne was sitting up in bed, and no longer prostrated on the pillows.

'I feel beastly. Where's Mother?'

'Marianne, dear, I'm afraid she'd gone out already when

[46]

I got down. Is there anything I can do to make you feel better?'

Marianne didn't, in fact, feel ill, but she did feel exceedingly cross, and this wasn't improved by hearing that her mother wasn't available, and remembering that she had gone for the better part of the day. She looked at Miss Chesterfield disagreeably. She felt in a mood to blame everyone for anything and it now seemed to her to be Miss Chesterfield's fault that Mark had given her roses and that her mother had gone out early and would be staying out late, and in fact for the whole miserable state of affairs.

'I don't want anything,' she said. 'I only want Mother to come home.'

'But we can't get hold of her yet, Marianne. Apparently she's going to visit an aunt of yours after lunch, so we could ring her up then, but she's not going to be anywhere near a telephone till then.'

'Then I don't want anything,' Marianne said miserably. She lay down in bed and hunched her shoulders. 'I wish I was dead, too,' she said.

'Do you feel very ill?' Miss Chesterfield said sympathetically.

'No. Yes. No.'

'Have you any pain anywhere? Or anything like you had before?'

'No,' said Marianne impatiently.

'Well,' said Miss Chesterfield practically, 'I can't judge how ill you are because I didn't see you before, when you were ill at first. So I'm going to ring up your doctor and he can decide.'

'I don't need a doctor,' Marianne said, very crossly indeed.

'I dare say you don't, but I can't take the risk of not sending for him, as your mother isn't here and I'm responsible for you. I'll go and telephone to him straight away and then, if you're up to it, I think you'd better do some work with me.'

She disappeared downstairs again. But the doctor was out on his rounds and wasn't easy to get hold of, and the best that his secretary could promise was that he would come along in the afternoon. Miss Chesterfield had to be content with this, and she came up and spent a tiresome and tiring morning trying to interest Marianne in history, French and English. She thoughtfully left out the tables of weights and measures which should have occupied the mathematics period, as being unsuitable to the feelings of either of them. But though, in the ordinary way, Marianne would have been interested in most of her work, she made herself stupid and inattentive this morning, and the hours dragged past, with Marianne closing her mind to everything that was said to her, and even Miss Chesterfield, in spite of her good resolutions, getting irritable. It was all the worse because Marianne knew she was being stupid and annoying, and that instead of providing Miss Chesterfield with a happy birthday, she was doing exactly the opposite. But she was powerless to help herself. She wanted to be clever and nice and much more likeable than the loathsome Mark, and yet every minute found her becoming stupider and ruder and more disagreeable.

When lunch came and released them both, Miss Chesterfield left with intense relief, and Marianne only waited till she was out of the room to burst into tears of rage and despair.

The doctor and her mother arrived nearly at the same moment later in the afternoon. Marianne had not been crying quite continuously till they came, but very nearly, and she felt ill with crossness and exhaustion. She hadn't eaten any lunch, which made her feel worse, and her official rest time had been spent in going over the day's events in her mind, an occupation not likely to soothe or refresh her.

Her mother was sympathetic and the doctor was grave. He told Marianne flatly that she was doing herself as much harm by getting into a state like that as she would by getting out of bed and running up and down stairs. She had sent her temperature up again and would probably need an extra week or so in bed.

'You can't help getting upset occasionally, nobody can,' he said reasonably, packing his small neat case at the end of Marianne's bed as he spoke. 'But for goodness' sake try not to get into a real state. Tell yourself it will all be the same in a hundred years or that there are as good fish in the sea as ever came out of it, or anything calming like that. Or just remember, which is the fact, that every time your temper or your temperature goes up one degree it means an extra day in bed. That ought to keep you cool.'

'It might when I'm all right, anyway,' Marianne pointed out. 'But when I'm really in a temper I don't think like that.'

'That's the trouble,' the doctor agreed. 'It's just when you need it most that you can't bring these things to mind. Anyway I'm giving you a new medicine to take today and for the rest of this week, which is guaranteed to prevent your getting even mildly irritated with anyone. And of course the better you feel, the less you'll want to be cross, so I dare say you won't be bothered again. Good-bye, Marianne. Remember – keep cool.'

He went. Marianne told her mother the whole story, which made her cry again, but this time with tears which were almost a relief, except that her face ached and her nose and eyes were sore, she had cried so much. She was quite extraordinarily tired, and the medicine left for her by the doctor – curious little capsules, very brilliantly coloured – made her even tireder. Long before her usual bedtime, she herself suggested that she should go to sleep, and it seemed as if the ordinary preparations for the night would never finish, her eyes were so heavy and her brain so weary.

At last the hair brushing, the face and hand washing, the straightening of the bed and the tidying up were over in a sort of distant haze. Marianne lay stretched in a cool un-ruffled bed, her mother opened the window and pulled the curtains, and before she had left the room Marianne was asleep.

Asleep, she dreamed.

7. Mark

It was very dark. Marianne could see a glimmer of light coming from what might be a heavily curtained window away up on her left, but it wasn't enough to enable her to see where she was. It felt like a room, cool but slightly stuffy, and what light there was looked as if it were coming in from outside.

Putting out an experimental hand Marianne touched a wall, smooth and firm. She moved her fingers along it, but the wall was not broken by furniture and seemed only to continue. She felt with her foot in front of her, and the ground seemed firm and even. She took a step, then another, feeling each time first. She was moving indirectly towards the glimmer of light and had nearly reached it, when the wall abruptly turned a corner, so that as her hand felt the angle, her foot kicked against the new bit of wall directly in front of her. This new wall led straight to the window or whatever it was: Marianne turned to walk with it and had only taken two or three steps, when the wall stopped and she was by the window. Her hand went out towards the bars of darkness – there were a great many of them – crossing the patch of faint light, but it did not reach them. Instead of wood or metal, which she had expected, her hand touched something warm, and quite definitely alive.

Marianne said, 'Oh!' in pure terror, and jumped backwards a foot or so.

A cross and sleepy voice said, 'What's the matter?'

There was a stir and a rustling between Marianne and the

window, and now her eyes had become accustomed to the darkness she could distinguish something moving. Somebody was stretching and sitting up just below the level of the window – perhaps on a couch or a bed pushed right up against the wall.

'Who's there?' the voice asked, and Marianne was encouraged to hear that it, too, sounded apprehensive.

'It's me,' said Marianne, as people so often do say in answer to this question. Then, realizing that it was not a complete answer, she added, 'I'm Marianne.'

There was a little sigh in the darkness, as if the questioner had relaxed with relief, and Marianne could see the person lean back against the embrasure of the wall. This seemed, at any rate, to show that whoever it was hadn't been lying in wait for her and might even be someone as frightened as she was. She said, in a rather uncertain voice, 'Who are you?'

'I'm Mark,' said the voice. It sounded slightly teasing now. 'Remember? We've met before, but you never got round to telling me your name.'

'How do you know, then?' Marianne asked. 'I mean how did you know it was me, if you didn't know my name last time? Can you see in the dark, or something like that?'

'I have X-ray eyes,' Mark said, in a piercing stage whisper. He added immediately in his ordinary voice, 'No, of course I can't, stupid. But I knew your voice directly you spoke. Besides you're the only person I ever see here, so I suppose I was half expecting it to be you.'

'But where is here? Where are we? How do you know where we are when it's so dark?'

'It got dark like this after I came. At least it was pretty dark at first, because of all the fastenings across the window, but it's got much darker outside since then. When I first got here I could see all round and recognize the place, but then I must have gone to sleep and it must have got dark. It's never been like this before.'

'I don't understand,' said Marianne, trying to be patient. 'Have you been here before?'

'Yes, and so have you.'

'I haven't. At least I don't recognize it. Where are we, Mark? I wish you'd explain.'

'It's the same old place, wherever that is. The house, you know, where we were before. It's the same room, from what I could see of it, and the same outside, I think, only I could hardly see that at all.'

'Why?'

'Because of the bars.'

'The bars?' Marianne repeated stupidly.

'The bars over the windows, silly! Can't you see, even now it's so dark? The whole window's covered with bars – there's hardly room to put your hand out.'

'I don't understand.'

'Nor do I. That makes two of us, doesn't it?' Mark's voice was not agreeable.

'Oh, don't be so beastly!' Marianne cried out, wretched. 'I can't bear it. You don't explain anything, and you keep on sort of laughing at me, and I hate it being dark and our not being able to see each other. It makes it much more frightening, and it's quite bad enough, anyway. Do stop.'

'I didn't know I'd begun,' said Mark nastily.

There was a short silence. Marianne could hear Mark breathing and her own heart beating, and somewhere, outside the room she supposed, the tick of a clock. Again she was reassured by that unhurried commonplace sound. It was presumably the same clock that she had heard and seen in the house last time she had been there, when she had found Mark in the empty room. But why had it suddenly become so dark and prison-like and why was he so horrid? She swallowed, and said, 'Mark?'

'Yes.'

'I'm sorry if I'm stupid, but I do wish you'd try to explain a bit more. I know you don't understand it all yourself,' she

[53]

said in a hurry, 'but at any rate you seem to know a lot more than I do, and you've been here longer, so you could tell me some things.'

'What do you want to know?' Mark asked, and he didn't sound exactly unfriendly.

'Well, first of all, is this the same room you were in last time I came?'

'Exactly the same. It's still well above ground level and it's still unfurnished. I've been sleeping on the window seat as you might have guessed.'

'It must be very uncomfortable,' said Marianne, eager to show that she could be sympathetic.

'It is. It's revolting. However, here I seem to be all the time, and here I obviously have to stay.'

'Why?' Marianne asked.

Mark shifted. 'I just have to,' he answered shortly. 'Anyhow, now I'm barred in.'

'Barred?'

'Yes. All those things across the window, are bars. And the up and down ones. It's the most extraordinary sort of barring I've ever seen – there's so much of it, it practically keeps out all the light, or what there is of it.'

'Can't you put a light on in here?' Marianne asked. 'Isn't there any electricity or something?'

'If there is I haven't found it,' the boy replied. 'There aren't any electric fittings, anyway.'

'And when you said 'now' – I don't quite understand. Did the bars just suddenly appear? They weren't here last time, were they? There was just window then, that you could have got through if you'd wanted to.'

'On the first floor,' Mark murmured.

'Well, you could have jumped,' Marianne protested. 'It's not very far up and only grass underneath.'

'You've forgotten something,' Mark said, and he sounded really disagreeable again now. 'I can't even walk, so I don't know how you suggest I should jump.'

'Oh, Mark, I'm sorry, I really am. I'd quite forgotten what you told me about your not being able to walk. It was awfully silly of me. I'm frightfully sorry.'

'All right,' Mark said briefly.

There was a short silence. Then Marianne began again.

'About the bars.'

'What about the bars?'

'I still don't quite understand. How did they come here? Who put them up? And why, anyway?'

'I don't know. They weren't here before, you're right about that, but how they got here is beyond me. Someone must have put them up from outside. And they're all uneven, too, not in straight lines, but higgledy-piggledy. Like a sort of mad scribble over the window, only in iron bars. What's the matter? What did you say?'

'It was a sort of noise, not exactly talking,' Marianne explained. 'Because I'd just thought of something.' She stopped.

'Well?'

Marianne hesitated.

'You'll probably think it's awfully silly.'

'I might,' Mark said encouragingly.

'But – well, I think it might have been me. That made the bars, you know. Because the house is all just exactly like what I drew. And then I came here, and here it was, only there wasn't anyone in it, and then I drew a face and the next time you were here, and this time I did a sort of scribble over the windows and there are the bars, so it probably was me, wasn't it?'

'I haven't', said Mark coldly and distantly, 'the remotest idea what you're talking about. It all sounds the most utter nonsense, if you want to know.'

'No, it isn't.' Marianne was so much excited that she ignored the coldness in Mark's voice, and feeling her way along the window seat to the end where his feet were, she sat down. 'Look, I'll begin at the beginning. I drew this house, in my drawing book, before I ever saw it. See? And the next time I dreamed I was here, outside it, looking at it, exactly as it was in my drawing. But I couldn't get in because there wasn't anyone inside it and there wasn't a knocker or anything on the door. And then I drew you looking out of the window, and the knocker on the door, and the next time I dreamed about it, they were both there – you and the knocker, I mean.'

'I don't see that that proves anything,' Mark objected. 'You could just as well say you dreamed about things after you'd drawn them, as that you made them come because you'd drawn them.'

'But you said yourself that first time there weren't any stairs, and then after I'd drawn the inside of the house and the stairs, they were there,' Marianne said triumphantly.

'They might have been there before,' Mark said.

'You said they weren't. You said you'd looked and there weren't any. And then after I'd drawn them and the rest of the inside of the house, they were there. And I was inside the house. And it's just like I drew it. And this time I did draw sort of scribbles across the window, and now they're there.'

She stopped, quite out of breath.

Mark said nothing.

'Well,' said Marianne impatiently. 'Don't you see? Surely you must believe it now?'

'No, I don't,' said Mark unexpectedly. 'It all sounds nonsense to me. You think you built this house and furnished it and put in stairs and rooms and things just by drawing pictures at home and then dreaming about them. What about me? Where do I come in? I suppose you think I shouldn't be here if you hadn't chosen to draw me in the first place?'

'No,' said Marianne boldly. 'I don't think you would.'

'Where would I be then? I suppose you think I shouldn't exist at all? You'll be saying next that I'm just part of your

[56]

dream and if you chose not to draw me or dream about me, I wouldn't be anywhere at all.'

'No,' said Marianne. 'I wouldn't say that because I know you do exist. Outside my dreaming about you, I mean. And anyway when I drew somebody to live in the house I didn't know it was going to be you. I just drew someone to have a person there. Only – I can't explain very well – I've got a sort of feeling that I couldn't draw things that weren't right to be here – I mean as if things that wouldn't fit in properly just wouldn't get drawn or would turn out looking like something else. So if I drew anyone, whatever it looked like, it would have to turn out to be you because somehow or other you're already here – I mean, you were here before I ever drew you, only I couldn't see you till I'd drawn it. Oh, don't you see, Mark?'

'Thanks,' said Mark stiffly. 'It's decent of you to allow that I may be a real person after all, and not just part of your scribblings.'

'Don't be beastly,' Marianne said, energetically. 'I always said I knew you were real. And, anyway, I was only explaining because of the bars. I'm afraid they probably are my fault – you see I was furious with you about the roses, you know, so I scribbled all over the window, and I'm afraid it's made bars. I'm very sorry – I didn't know or I'd have been more careful.'

'Oh, shut up,' Mark said. 'Don't be so beastly apologetic and so sure you've done everything. You seem to think this world belongs to you and that everything that happens here happens because you've made it. I don't believe it, anyway. Look at you – you're only a little girl. You aren't all that clever. Why you can't do anything about it now you are here – you can't get us out of here and you can't make it light again. You're no better off than I am except that you can walk and I can't. If I could, I wouldn't be here long, I can tell you. But you – you come here in the dark and you want me to tell you all about the place and where we are and who we are and everything, and then when I've told you all I know, you start saying you made it all happen and you invented this and made that. You want to run the whole show, that's what you want, pretending it's all part of your beastly little drawings.'

'It is!' Marianne said. She was furious.

'All right, then, prove it! Go and draw something useful with that drawing book. Draw us both outside the beastly house, or get me walking again. Then I'll believe you. But you can't, and you know you can't. You're showing off. Just like a girl.' He spoke with bitter contempt.

'All right,' said Marianne. 'I will show you. First of all I'll rub you out so I never have to see you again, and then I'll scribble over the whole house so it's dark all the time and you'll never get out, and then I'll stop dreaming about you and you'll die! You'll be dead if I won't dream about you, and I won't! There won't be any house and there won't be any you and then perhaps you'll believe me.' She knew that what she was saying didn't make sense, but she was far too angry to care.

'Try,' said the boy, and the disbelief in his voice was the final insult.

'All right,' Marianne answered. She stood up. 'I won't dream,' she said. 'I won't, I won't, I won't! I'm not here, there isn't a house, there isn't a room with me in it and Mark, there's nothing but me. I'm in bed, dreaming. I'm going to wake up. This is a dream and I'm going to wake up.'

She woke. It was morning, and outside the dull windows summer rain dripped steadily as it had dripped all through the night.

8. Mark in Danger

Marianne, when she was properly awake, felt almost as angry and miserable as she had in the dream. She sat up in bed and pulled the bedside table towards her so that she could reach her drawing book. She opened it at the drawing of the house and looked at it again.

'I can make things happen there,' she said to herself. 'I did before. The lines I drew across the windows are exactly like the bars there. I'll get rid of Mark. I won't ever see him there again.'

She had picked up an india-rubber and had started trying to rub out the face at the window before she remembered that the pencil was apparently an indelible one, and couldn't be rubbed out. Sure enough all her rubbing had no effect except to make the paper rough and dirty.

'I'll get rid of him somehow,' she thought. She took her thickest and blackest black crayon and scribbled busily over the lower part of the window. Soon there was no face looking out: only the black window. On the opposite page she did the same over the little figure in the upper room in the inside view of the house.

'I won't have that beastly Mark,' Marianne said, 'I'll have someone else – I'll have a little girl – I'll have Fiona!' Fiona was the one of the six little chicken-pox girls she had felt most attracted to, probably because she had also been ten when Miss Chesterfield had taught them, and had been, Miss Chesterfield said, very pretty.

She drew, in one of the downstairs rooms, a little girl. She came out rather too big for the room, owing to Marianne's attention to detail in her clothes: she gave her to wear everything she most hankered after herself, including proper riding breeches and riding boots, and – as a great refinement – spurs.

'Oh dear, if I ever do meet her she'll be a sort of giantess,' Marianne thought disconsolately, looking at her picture. 'But perhaps I shall be too, so as to fit. I'm sure she'll be nice and believe in my being able to do things by drawing, and then if she likes I'll draw a whole lot of horses and we can ride on them in my dreams. I expect she could teach me. If she can ride herself, at least. But she ought to be able to if she's got proper riding breeches. I wonder if I could draw her somehow or other so she looked as if she was a frightfully good rider already? Perhaps if I drew her just a tiny little bit bow-legged like jockeys are supposed to be –'

She was contemplating this happy idea when the door opened and her mother came in.

'How are you this morning?' she began, but when she saw Marianne's bed already strewn with crayons and pencils and paper, she said quickly, 'Oh, Marianne, what a mess! Already! And here's your breakfast arriving. We'll have to clear up very quickly and really tidy out this room today. It's getting disgracefully piled up – there isn't room to move.'

She managed to make room for the breakfast tray by bundling everything on the bed off on to the bookcase: and after the breakfast for which Marianne, feeling strangely tired, was much less hungry than usual, her mother came up and did a little perfunctory tidying before Miss Chesterfield's arrival, promising that in the afternoon she would come up and spend a long time there and really make the room more like a room to be lived in and less like an old junk shop.

Meeting Miss Chesterfield was embarrassing after the incidents of the day before, but not as embarrassing as it would have been if Marianne hadn't known that Miss Chesterfield knew nothing except that she had felt ill yesterday and was better today. She felt sleepy and slow, however, which she was told was the result of the new medicine she was taking, and although Miss Chesterfield made every allowance for this, she couldn't help being irritated sometimes by Marianne's inattention, and showing her annoyance. Altogether it was not a very successful morning and Marianne was glad when it was over.

'And now lunch, and then I go to Mark,' Miss Chesterfield said, as cheerfully as she could, as she put away the books they had been using. Marianne's suspicious ear heard in her tone the suggestion that going to teach Mark would be a pleasant change from Marianne.

'You went to see Mark yesterday as well,' she objected.

'That was extra. I always go on Thursdays,' Miss Chesterfield replied, 'and Fridays and Mondays. And you know that quite well, Marianne, so don't pretend you've forgotten. I'm expecting to find Mark rather cross this afternoon because I told him yesterday he'd got to learn some poetry for a change.'

'A change from what?' Marianne couldn't help asking, though she didn't really want to hear anything about Mark.

'Oh, from arithmetic problems, and Latin exercises and geometry and that sort of thing. He's a clever boy, Mark, and he'll lap up all the more difficult stuff without turning a hair. But things like poetry get rather left out, and he doesn't like being made to stop being clever and just listen.'

'But I thought you said he was lazy.'

'Not in his work. Perhaps about trying to do things he doesn't do well straight off, like learning to walk again, poor boy. Good-bye, Marianne. I must fly. I hope you feel better tomorrow.'

Marianne did feel better the next day. The medicine, although so brightly coloured, certainly seemed to have a calming effect. She felt dull sometimes, but not cross, and although it was maddening to feel that she had added on to the length of her stay in bed by losing her temper, she didn't

feel any the worse for the outbreak after a day or two. The days went smoothly by – her room looked a great deal tidier and she and her mother made a great many good resolutions about not letting it get so littered up again. But as Marianne was embarking on patchwork as a useful way of passing the time, these resolutions didn't seem very likely to be strictly kept.

Rather to Marianne's surprise, she had no dreams. But this suited her. She wanted to forget Mark and it was easier if she could also forget the house and her dream and everything to do with him. She was also in no great hurry to meet a giant Fiona in riding breeches.

It was about a week after the great row that Miss Chesterfield was late again. Not nearly as late as she had been the first time, only about five or ten minutes late, in fact, and Marianne had hardly noticed that it was after her usual time of arrival when she came in.

'I'm sorry I'm late,' she said at once. 'I had to call in on the way here at –' She stopped.

Something in her voice made Marianne take especial

notice. She said immediately, 'You went to see Mark.'

'Yes. At least, not Mark himself. But I did go to his house.'

'Why didn't you see him, then?' Marianne asked suspiciously.

'Because he's not there.'

'Has he gone away?' Marianne asked, pleased that Mark should be well out of Miss Chesterfield's way.

'Yes.' Miss Chesterfield hesitated, and then said, 'He's in hospital.'

'In hospital? Why?'

'He caught a cold and it got much worse and he had to go to hospital for special treatment.'

'Just for a cold!' Marianne said scornfully. She thought to herself that Mark must be a miserable mollycoddle if he had to go to hospital to be nursed for something as ordinary as a cold.

'It started by being a cold, but then he got bronchitis and pneumonia and, you see, some of the muscles he can't use properly yet are the muscles you breathe with, so it's very dangerous if he gets any sort of infection in his lungs and he has to go into hospital where they've got the right sort of apparatus to help him to breathe.'

'Dangerous?' said Marianne, suddenly alarmed.

'Yes, I'm afraid so,' Miss Chesterfield said. 'That's why I went round to see his parents this morning, to ask what the news was. He went into hospital two days ago and I wanted to hear what the latest report said.'

'You mean really dangerous? Like dying? He isn't going to die, is he, Miss Chesterfield?'

'I hope not,' Miss Chesterfield said, but she didn't sound very hopeful. 'They say there's quite a chance that he may be all right, but they just can't tell yet.'

'But there's all sorts of things they could try,' Marianne urged. 'Penicillin and that sort of thing, that cures everything.'

'I'm sure they're doing everything they can,' Miss Chesterfield said. She looked at Marianne anxiously. 'You mustn't worry,' she said. 'After all, you don't know Mark. I shouldn't be making you anxious, only I couldn't help telling you as I've told you so much about him before. But don't worry, Marianne. It's a very good hospital and he's got one of the best doctors in the country and I expect he'll be all right. After all, they do say there's quite a chance he'll recover.'

'But –' Marianne began, but Miss Chesterfield interrupted her.

'I think we'd better not go on talking about it, Marianne,' she said. 'It will only be upsetting for both of us. And we've got plenty of work to do, without discussing something that doesn't depend on us. Show me your composition homework.'

Marianne, reluctantly, had to agree. But she found it very difficult to think about her lessons. Her mind would keep wandering away to Mark in hospital, Mark in one of those breathing machines – she had seen pictures of them – Mark perhaps dying now, this minute – and all because of her.

Miss Chesterfield said it was something that didn't depend on them, Marianne and herself. But didn't it? Marianne remembered uncomfortably, miserably, that she had told Mark in the dream that she would stop dreaming about him and he would die. And she had stopped dreaming. And she had said she would scribble his face out of her pictures, and she had. She had blacked out Mark, out of her house, out of her dream life, out of her mind. And now he was dying, perhaps this minute he was already dead.

But wasn't this doing just what Mark himself had accused her of – making herself too important? If it really was Mark she had dreamed about, the real live Mark whom Miss Chesterfield taught and who had a home and parents and a life quite apart from her dreams about him, was it likely that he would just cease to exist because she stopped dreaming about him? Or die because she made black marks on a picture? It didn't seem possible – and yet it had all happened

[64]

just at the right time – it all fitted in horribly well.

'Oh, I *don't* understand,' Marianne said, and she said it aloud, in her grief and despair. Miss Chesterfield, who was waiting for her to finish working out a complicated sum in long division, looked up.

'What don't you understand? It's not really so very difficult, it's just laborious. Can I explain anything to make it clearer?'

'No,' Marianne said drearily, 'thank you. I expect I'll be able to do it soon – but I don't feel awfully clever this morning, Miss Chesterfield. I can't help thinking about Mark, though I know you don't want us to talk about him.'

Miss Chesterfield simply said, 'No,' which might have been an answer to any part of what Marianne had said. But she did explain the sum to Marianne, and made her do the working out aloud, which made it easier to concentrate, and then very soon afterwards she left, saying she would try not to be late the next day and hoped she'd be able to bring better news.

When she had gone, Marianne lay and thought. She couldn't make up her mind about Mark, whether she was responsible for his illness or not. She felt sure that if she suggested that she was responsible to anyone else, any grown-up person especially, they would say that it was a ridiculous idea and would think she was being self-important and silly.

'And yet he was a real person in my dream,' Marianne thought, 'and I was beastly to him. And he was beastly to me,' she added honestly. 'But it does seem awfully queer that he should start being ill just when I'd done that to my picture of him and said I wouldn't dream about him and that I wished he was dead and all that.'

She felt guilty about it. Even if it wasn't at all her fault, she felt miserable, and exactly as if she had done her best to kill Mark.

Suddenly she had what seemed a brilliant idea.

'If I could make him ill by scribbling over him I could make him better by doing the opposite. Only I can't rub that pencil out. Bother! But perhaps I could do something to make it go, or draw another picture or have a different kind of dream. After all, if I can make bad things happen I ought to be able to make good things happen just as much. I'll draw a picture of Mark feeling quite well again. Only I suppose then I'll have to dream about him again, and I don't want to. I don't see why I should have to dream about him – why can't he get well without my having to see him? Perhaps I could just draw him looking quite well, but not in that house, which is where I always seem to get to. And then he probably wouldn't believe I'd done anything about it, he'd think it had all just happened, and what I'd done didn't make any difference at all!'

She stopped to consider this. Although she definitely didn't want Mark to die, particularly didn't want to feel that his death was in any way connected with what she did or didn't do, she also didn't want Mark alive and cocky and sneering, in her dreams, telling her that she was no use and hadn't any influence on what happened to him.

'Bother,' said Marianne to herself. 'I suppose I'll have to draw him getting well. Even if he doesn't believe it's anything to do with me when he is quite better. But I wish I could prove it somehow. Only I'll have to get him well first – I can't just let him get worse and die, even if he is beastly when he's well again.'

Once she had decided this she felt she must hurry up. She had gathered from Miss Chesterfield that Mark was indeed dangerously ill. He might die, Marianne felt, at any moment, and if there was really anything she could do to save him, she must do it, and do it at once.

She turned to her bedside table for the drawing book.

It was not there.

She remembered that the day after the row her mother had come in and tidied up the whole room. The drawing book must have been put away somewhere, she had no idea where.

Nor, when she asked, had her mother.

Marianne, frantic, insisted that the book must be found. She must have it as soon as possible. Her mother couldn't remember what it looked like, couldn't recognize Marianne's rather incoherent descriptions, couldn't recollect having seen anything like a drawing book for weeks. She searched and Marianne's feverish eyes searched with her. The afternoon turned into evening and the evening into night. Mark was in hospital, he was desperately ill, probably dying and it might all be Marianne's fault. She couldn't retrieve it without her drawing book. And the drawing book was not to be found.

9. Marianne and Mark

Marianne slept badly that night. She kept on waking and realizing that she hadn't dreamed, determining that this time she would, she must dream, and then half sleeping again. Towards morning she did dream, but not about the house and not about Mark. She dreamed that she was lame and couldn't walk without a crutch. It was terribly important to get somewhere in time, an appointment, a train to catch, she wasn't sure what, but she couldn't hurry because she had lost her crutch and though she looked everywhere for it, she couldn't find it and the time was getting shorter and shorter. She woke out of breath and anxious, and her mother, coming in to say good morning to her, exclaimed instead, 'Marianne, what is the matter? Didn't you sleep well?'

'Not very,' Marianne said. She felt terrible. Her head ached, her eyes were hot and heavy, she felt stupid and worried.

'Has Miss Chesterfield come yet?' she asked.

'Good heavens, no! It's only just eight o'clock – I know we're late but we're not that late. Wake up,' her mother said. 'You're still asleep, Marianne. Come on, my love, sit up and let me brush your hair. You'll feel better when you've had some breakfast and if you're very sleepy this afternoon you can have an extra sleep then.'

'When will Miss Chesterfield arrive do you think?' Marianne asked several times during her morning hair-brushing and washing and cleaning of teeth.

'About the usual time, I should imagine,' her mother said briskly, each time she asked. 'Half past nine or a minute or two later, perhaps. Why?'

'I just wondered,' Marianne said feebly.

But when Miss Chesterfield did ring the front doorbell and Marianne heard the sort of subdued bustle that goes on in the hall as someone takes off their coat, hangs up their umbrella and so on, she could hardly wait till Miss Chesterfield had got into her room before she had burst out with, 'How's Mark?' She hadn't meant to come out with it like that, as if she'd been thinking of nothing else since she'd seen Miss Chesterfield last, even though that was the case, but she couldn't help herself.

Miss Chesterfield hesitated.

'He's no worse,' she said at last, but not in a very cheerful voice.

'Better?' urged Marianne.

'No. Not exactly. I suppose he's just about the same.'

'Is he still in that lung thing – that machine?' Marianne asked.

'Oh, yes. He'll be in that for some time, I should think, even if – even when he's better. It helps him to breathe, you see, and though his breathing muscles are getting stronger, this illness will hold him up a bit – he'll have to be careful for a time afterwards.'

'He is going to be all right, isn't he?'

'No one can say yet, Marianne. But now stop talking about Mark and get on with your poetry.'

Marianne did as she was told, though she privately thought Miss Chesterfield was rather unfeeling. However, in a way it was a relief to have to think about something different and to be made to attend to her lessons. Her brain was tired with worrying over the problem of Mark and her responsibility for his illness, and she was quite pleased at the end of the morning to realize that she hadn't had time to think much about him. But she was tired all over. Her back ached, her arms ached, her legs ached and her head ached. She mentioned this to her mama when she came up with Marianne's lunch on a tray.

[69]

'A rest this afternoon, then,' her mother said. 'You look tired too, Marianne, and you didn't have a good night. You must lie down and try to sleep after lunch and then you'll be able to enjoy the evening.'

Marianne felt as if she would never be able to enjoy anything again, but she was really too tired to protest, and after lunch she let her mother remove her 'sitting-up' pillows and smooth her sheets, and actually felt pleased to be lying flat and straight in the bed.

'I probably shan't go to sleep,' she said grudgingly, as her mother firmly pulled the curtains. 'But it is nice to lie down.'

'Well, don't stay awake just to prove to me that you aren't sleepy,' her mother said, laughing, as she left the room.

And immediately Marianne felt her eyelids closing by themselves. She didn't just go to sleep – she dropped thousands of feet into sleep, with the rapidity and soundless perfection of a gannet's dive. It was completely satisfying and quite inescapable.

At once she was in the house. She hadn't meant to be – she hadn't had time to think about dreaming. But she was there, standing at the bottom of the stairs again, with the quiet, familiar tick of the clock above telling her that this was indeed where she had been before.

'So the clock's still here,' Marianne thought. She tried to remember just what she had done in her last drawing which would make a difference to her surroundings.

She had blacked out Mark's window. She had scribbled out Mark. And in one of the downstairs rooms she had put the little giantess, Fiona.

'I suppose she's in that one,' Marianne thought rather fearfully, glancing towards the door of the room in which she had first found herself.

She listened. There were no sounds except for the friendly tick of the clock overhead.

'I ought to be brave,' Marianne said to herself. 'After all, she won't hurt me. And probably the things here don't really come out just the size I draw, but the right sort of sizes, like they would be if I was a really good artist and drew properly. I don't expect I drew Mark or the clock or anything quite exactly right, but they've come out quite proper, not too large or small or anything.'

She took an indecisive step towards the door.

'I wanted her to play with me,' she reminded herself. 'She has riding breeches.' Somehow this didn't seem quite as attractive now as it had when she drew it.

'There's no Mark upstairs,' she thought. The house felt lonely directly she remembered this. She walked as boldly as she could to the door of the room where Fiona was waiting for her, a miniature giantess, booted and spurred, and opened the door very quickly.

The room was empty. It was absolutely bare, just as it had been when Marianne had first seen it.

She looked, half in amazement, half in relief.

'I must have got the rooms the wrong way round,' she thought. 'It must be the one on the other side of the front door.'

She left the room she was in and crossed the hall. After only a moment's indecision outside the second door, she opened that, too.

This room was as bare and empty as the first. No big little girl, no furniture, not so much as a hair from a horse's tail to show that there had ever been anything like Marianne's conception of the horse-riding Fiona in the place.

A new sudden hope sprang up in Marianne. She ran out of the room, banging the door behind her, and up the stairs, two at a time. Her feet clattered on the stone, and echoed in the empty house, but she was too eager to notice. She flung open the door at the top of the stairs.

The room was darker than on the first occasion when she had seen it, but not as absolutely black as on her last visit. Daylight came in between the stout bars outside the window. And there, on the window seat, stretched out and motionless, was Mark.

Marianne's first feeling was only relief that Mark was actually here, that her vicious scribblings hadn't done away with him. Her next feeling was fear because he was so still. Supposing she had not done away with him, but somehow killed him? She didn't know what she could or couldn't do in this house, how much what happened was or wasn't her fault, and now she didn't know what had happened to Mark.

She said, experimentally, 'Mark!' Immediately he half sat up, and turned to look at her, leaning on one elbow.

'Hullo,' he said, 'it's you. I thought you weren't ever coming back.'

'I didn't think I'd want to,' Marianne said awkwardly. She hesitated in the doorway.

'Well, come in properly, if you are coming in,' Mark said impatiently. 'And shut the door. I'm cold.'

'But it's summer!' said Marianne in surprise. She came right into the room and shut the door, however.

'Well, I can be cold in summer if I like,' Mark said. 'And anyhow your beastly bars keep most of the sun out of this room.'

'They aren't my bars.'

'Well, you seemed to be feeling responsible for them last time we met,' he reminded her.

'But, Mark, I don't understand. I did draw bars across the window once, and then next time I was here, they were there, like they are now. But I've drawn some other things, since then, and they aren't.'

'Aren't what?'

'Aren't here.'

'Well, why should they be? Do you expect everything you draw to appear here?' Mark looked scornfully round the empty room. 'If so, all I can say is, you must be a very good hand at drawing nothing.'

Marianne kept her temper by a miracle. To give herself time to recover she went over to the window seat and looked out of the window. The fence round the garden was certainly higher than when she had seen it last, and she wondered rather miserably what might be waiting outside it. And the bars were most certainly there on the window. Why then hadn't Mark disappeared, and why was there no Fiona?

She turned to look at Mark. Now she was close to him she was shocked at his appearance. He looked ill, heavy-eyed, as if he hadn't slept properly for days, and remarkably thin. He was watching her, frowning slightly, but as if he were puzzled rather than cross, and for some reason this made Marianne suddenly feel much warmer towards him than she ever had before.

'I wish you'd explain it to me, Mark,' she said, forgetting her hostility towards him and knowing somehow that if he could understand something she couldn't, he would feel more kindly towards her.

'Explain what?' Mark asked, but he didn't sound unfriendly.

'Why some of the things I've drawn do appear here and others don't. I know you're going to say I'm conceited or pleased with myself about my drawing,' she hurriedly added. 'But I'm not, honestly I'm not. Only such a lot of the things here are exactly like what I draw, only better of course, and then the bars appeared and the fence round the garden has got much higher, and I did draw that. But then last time I drew some things that just aren't here at all, so I don't understand.'

'Look,' said Mark, 'start at the beginning. You keep on talking about how you drew this and you drew that and then they appeared or you found them, and I don't know what it's all about. When did you start drawing, anyway, and what's it all got to do with this?'

'Well, you know this isn't ordinary life? I mean we're not always here, are we?'

'I don't know,' Mark said slowly. 'The thing is I can't remember much at all. I don't feel as if I'd always been here and never anywhere else, or as if I'd always been – I mean, I think I used to be quite well and I could move about all right. But I can't remember it, see? It's as if I felt I'd been ordinary and lived somewhere else for a lot of the time, but I can't think where I was or when I was well, so it looks as if I'd always been here and just imagined the other, or something.'

'Can't you remember anything?' Marianne asked.

'Not really. Not about anything different from here. I remember you being here before, twice. And last time you got very angry and said you wished I was dead – no, you said if you didn't dream I would be dead.' He stopped for a moment, and then said in a different voice, 'Why did you say dream?'

'I think I thought if I didn't dream about you, you wouldn't be here,' Marianne said lamely. She felt rather muddled herself.

'But this – this isn't a dream,' Mark protested. 'This is real.'

'Yes, it is, isn't it?' Marianne agreed. She couldn't remember why she had been so sure then that she was dreaming. Now it seemed to her that this house, this time, this boy, were as real as anything she had ever known, and yet she knew also that there was another life, an ordinary life, which went on at the same time as this one, but in a different place, and with different people, and that she belonged to both lives and both belonged to her.

'Mark!' she said.

'Yes, what?'

'Even if you're always here, I'm not.'

'So I've noticed,' said Mark.

'Yes, but when I'm not here, in this room, I mean, I'm not just somewhere else in the house. Or outside or anything. I'm somewhere quite different. It's more ordinary, somehow. Things couldn't happen there like they do here – the bars and the fence, for instance.'

'Well?' said Mark. 'What's all that got to do with me and you drawing the bars and everything?'

'Because it's in the other life I do the drawing. And when I'm there, that seems real. Realer than this. When I'm there, this seems like a dream.'

'Go on.'

'Well, it was there I found the pencil and drew this house. And then I came here and it was just like my drawing – just a field and grass and the house and no one in it. And I felt I'd got to get in but I couldn't unless there was someone there. And when I was at home again and I drew you, and a knocker on the door, and then the next time I came here, you were here and so was the knocker. Don't you remember? And then the stairs, I drew them, and the rooms and you in this one?'

She stopped, out of breath.

'You draw them – and then what?' Mark asked. 'How do you know you don't draw them after you've been here – remembering them? Not before?'

'I couldn't prove it,' Marianne said. 'But I do know. I drew the knocker on the door so that I could get into the house, because the first time I came there wasn't one and I couldn't make anyone hear. And I drew you.'

'You didn't invent me,' Mark said, firmly but not unkindly.

'No, I know I didn't. Mark, don't be angry with me, but there's something I must tell you.'

'What?'

'In my ordinary sort of world – the realer life, you know – well, you're there.'

'I don't remember,' Mark said angrily, 'I told you I couldn't remember – I've seen you here before, I told you that, but I've never seen you anywhere else. You're inventing.'

'I'm not,' said Marianne indignantly. 'There's no reason why I should invent anything about you.'

'Then why say we've met in this other life of yours when I'm positive we haven't?'

'We haven't met. I just know you're there. I've heard about you – lots about you.'

'How?'

'From Miss Chesterfield. Oh, Mark, do think hard. Do try to remember. You must know Miss Chesterfield. She teaches us – you and me – only separately. She goes to your home to teach you and she comes to my home and teaches me – surely you know her, you must remember?'

Mark frowned.

'I somehow feel I've heard the name, that's all. Look, Marianne, I don't exactly not believe you, but it all seems so frightfully unlikely. Why on earth should this Miss Chester-whatever-she-is teach me at home? Why shouldn't I go to school? Is she a sort of governess? Because I'm much too old for that.'

'She's not a proper governess, not the ordinary kind. She goes round teaching children who've been ill and who can't go to school.'

'Are you ill, then?' Mark asked carefully.

'Yes. At least I was, in this other life, I was. Then I got better, but I'm still kept in bed, and Miss Chesterfield comes to teach me till I'm well enough to go back to school.'

'What about me?' Mark asked, very casually.

'Yes, you've been ill, too,' Marianne said as gently as she could.

'But now I'm better?'

'Yes. At least you were. Just this very moment you're a bit bad again.'

'How bad? In bed? Of course this is all in your imagination, you know.'

'You're in hospital,' Marianne said. She didn't know how to say it kindly enough. 'Mark, I think why you can't remember anything about ordinary life, the other life you know, is because you're ill there. I think if you were quite well there, or getting better, or something like that, you'd remember here about there. I'm sure you did before.'

'Am I badly ill?' Mark asked. 'You may as well tell me the truth, you know. Am I in hospital because I'm going to die?'

Marianne hesitated.

'Go on,' the boy said. 'Tell me. Am I supposed to be dying?'

He sat up on the window seat and looked hard at Marianne, with those tired, heavy eyes. His skin was pale, much paler and not so freckled as it had been the first time she had seen him. She knew that in spite of his apparently casual air and his asking her this question as ordinarily as if he had been asking her what the weather was like outside, he was frightened, and she must reassure him.

'No,' she said, and she didn't care at that moment whether what she said was true or not. 'No, you're not going to die. I don't know whether you're supposed to be dying or not, but you're not going to. I know you're not.'

'Is that another of the things you know or are you going to draw it to make certain?' he asked. But she could feel that he was relieved by her certainty.

'I can't draw it,' Marianne admitted. 'If I could I would, but I can't find the book. But I don't need to draw this, Mark, I'm sure without drawing. I know you'll get well. You must believe that I know it, Mark. You're going to get well, you're going to get well. I know you are.'

She felt, as she said it, that it was true. Mark was lying back now, looking at her and she couldn't make out from his expression what he was thinking. But it seemed more important than anything had before in all the world that he should believe her now.

Suddenly he gave her a not unfriendly smile.

'You're mad,' he said, quite kindly. 'Getting so het up about nothing. Of course I know I'm not dying. After all I can see I'm not, can't I? I'll be perfectly all right as soon as I don't feel so tired. Still, it's nice of you to mind so much, even if it is all your imagination.'

'It isn't,' Marianne began indignantly. 'You'll soon see it isn't when you wake up in hospital and find you've really been ill and –'

She stopped.

'You look awfully tired,' she said abruptly.

'Sorry, I'm afraid I am. It's perfectly true I do feel rotten – not ill, of course, just frightfully tired, as if I'd done an awful lot, though of course I haven't.'

'Go to sleep,' Marianne advised.

'Perhaps I will,' Mark said unexpectedly.

He stretched out on the window seat. 'Beastly hard this place is,' he grumbled agreeably, 'I'm sometimes surprised I ever manage to go to sleep. If you're so clever at making things suddenly appear here, what about a bed and a blanket or two?'

'I'll try,' said Marianne, wondering if she would ever find her drawing book again.

'Thank you for nothing,' said Mark's voice, teasing but sleepy. 'And I could do with some books – and some games – and my bike – oh, no, I suppose it wouldn't be much use

to me up here – and some decent food – and – Marianne –'
  'Yes, Mark?'
  But although she waited before she woke up for his next remark, it didn't come, because Mark, in the dream, had fallen asleep.

10. The Pencil

It occurred to Marianne that Mark's tiredness almost seemed to be catching, as even after she had slept in the afternoon she was tired herself, and it wasn't until the following morning that she felt at all better, and able to consider what was to be done. She had been so sleepy the previous evening that she hadn't seriously begun to look for her drawing book, but this morning, sitting up in bed and feeling suddenly almost energetically well, she knew that she must find it and must draw in it some of the things Mark wanted. He had looked so very uncomfortable sleeping on that window seat.

'And I've got to make him better,' Marianne thought. 'Only I don't know how to draw him getting better.'

But she felt sure he was getting better, whether she drew it or not. Something about their conversation in the last dream, the way in which he had appeared to be convinced and had gone to sleep, made her certain, as certain as she could be without actually hearing it, that he wasn't going to die.

She lay in bed and looked round. Her window looked east and this morning the room was full of bright sunlight, printing a pattern of brown and gold on the wall and turning the air into strips of dancing bright dust. If she leant on her elbow Marianne could see out of her window, a church steeple, very bright bluey-grey in the sunlight, shining silver slate roofs of houses and the trembling grey-green leaves of an aspen poplar in the garden of the big house that backed on to her home. The leaves of that poplar were never still:

even when there seemed to be no wind at all and all the other trees were motionless, the poplar's leaves stirred and rustled, making a soft whispering noise indistinguishable from a summer shower. They were moving now, looking new minted in the early sun.

Marianne looked at the picture on her wall, the only picture in the room, of a ship, a yacht with white sails, on a very green sea with white tips to the waves. She liked the picture because it had only sea and sky and the yacht in it – no land, no birds, no fish, just the clean white of the yacht and the green of the frothing waves. It was a cool picture to look at if you felt hot, and an out-of-door, wind-blown picture to feel if the room seemed stuffy.

She looked at her curtains which had originally been blue with a small climbing grey leaf all over them and occasional orange berries: but they had faded so much in the sun, in spite of the maker's guarantee, that now they were a sort of dull greyish-blue all over, rather pretty, but quite unlike they had been when bought.

She looked at her bed. Over the top of her blanket her mother had put a thin woollen covering known in the family as 'Joseph' because it had so many colours. It had been knitted by various people, and it was made of different coloured squares of ends of wool. Marianne was fond of it. She had loved it since she was very small and had spent hours choosing one colour after another as her favourite. The squares hadn't all come out the same size, and the whole rug had a curious lop-sided effect as it was pulled sideways by the unevenness of the sizes of square.

Marianne's eyes slid up a ray of sun to her bookcase. They ran over the backs of the books while her mind considered the insides. There were some she must get rid of, she was too old for them now. There were one or two which she'd never properly read, they were so difficult to get started on – *Hereward the Wake*, *Lorna Doone*, *The Daisy Chain*. She thought she might enjoy them if only she could have read half the book before she began, but they were terribly stiff to begin and to get into the middle of.

Next to *The Daisy Chain*, which was a dark blue book with gilt lettering, was a thin orange book – *The King of the Golden River*. Then came *The Cuckoo Clock*, grey and black. Then a taller paper-backed book, so thin it was almost invisible between two fatter books –

'My drawing book!' Marianne exclaimed inside herself, 'But we looked everywhere for it, at least Mother did. And now it's there, right in front of me. I could have seen it all the time! How extraordinary!'

She felt enormously relieved. Although she couldn't reach the book without getting out of bed, which was forbidden, she felt happy at just knowing where it was. She lay and looked at it, secure in the knowledge that she could have it when she wanted it, and could draw things that Mark wanted and make him a good deal more comfortable, as well as proving to him, by doing so, that she really had the power to make things appear in the house. She lay comfortably considering this until she went to sleep again and only awoke to find her breakfast being brought into the room by her mother.

With the drawing book propped up in front of her, Marianne ate toast and marmalade and boiled egg with great satisfaction. The only thing she didn't like was seeing her own enraged efforts at eliminating Mark from the pictures. It was all very well to want to make him more comfortable now, but she had certainly done all she could to get rid of him last time she had had the book.

'I wonder if the pencil really is indelible?' she thought, 'I'll try with my best india-rubber, the big squashy one, and see if that makes any difference.'

So directly she had finished her breakfast she tried to rub out the bars across the windows, the frantic scribbles over Mark, the rather unpleasant-looking Fiona in the downstairs room, and the one-eyed stones outside the garden wall.

She discovered a most extraordinary thing.

Some of the drawings disappeared most satisfactorily under the rubber. Others stayed as clear and firm as ever.

Fiona went and left no trace: the scribbles on top of Mark vanished, too, in both pictures, leaving Mark's face at the window, and the small figure in the upstairs room as before. But the bars in front of the windows, the heightened fence and the sinister stones outside she could not move. She could undo some of her drawing, but not all.

This was very puzzling. Marianne sat and looked at the drawing book for several minutes before any solution to the puzzle occurred to her. Then she turned to look at her pencils, lying in an open box on her bedside table, and suddenly she *saw*.

When she had drawn the house first, and then the door knocker and Mark's face at the window, she had used The Pencil. The Pencil that had come out of great-grandmother's workbox. And when she had drawn the bars and the stones outside the garden, and the hills and the road, she had again used The Pencil. But when she had scribbled out Mark and drawn in Fiona she had used one of her own ordinary crayons, and what she had drawn with that had not only proved to be delible, or whatever the opposite to indelible is, but had also *not* appeared in the dream.

'So it's the pencil!' Marianne thought in surprise. 'It's the pencil that started it all!'

Of course. Because she had never dreamed about what she had drawn before, she had never before gone back into the same dream again so consistently, she had never before been able to make things happen in a dream by drawing them in waking life. She remembered how she had had her very first dream about the house on the same day that she had found the pencil. And she had recognized it as a very special pencil the first moment she had set eyes on it.

She turned anxiously to the box by her bed. It would be terrible if now, just when she had learnt the value of the pencil, it had vanished like her drawing book. But she was immediately relieved to see it there, among other more ordinary crayons and pencils and ball-point pens, looking just as attractively drawable-with and yet undistinguished, a lovable but not an outstanding pencil, as ever.

'And now,' thought Marianne, picking up The Pencil, turning to a fresh sheet of her drawing book and rapidly drawing in the outline of a room, which was to be an enlargement of Mark's room in the house, 'I'll give Mark all the things he needs to be comfortable.'

But she hadn't got further than the rough top and legs of a table, when she heard Miss Chesterfield's voice on the stairs. Although she felt she knew the answer, although today's voice alone would have been enough to tell her, it was so different from yesterday's voice, so gay and happy, yet Marianne had a moment of sick fear and her heart actually gave an extra little hop, a most uncomfortable feeling, when Miss Chesterfield opened the door and Marianne, without at all knowing she was going to, had said immediately, 'How's Mark?'

'Oh, much better. Much, much better,' Miss Chesterfield said. 'He's going to be all right, they think.'

'Think?' Marianne echoed in horrified surprise. 'Don't they know yet?'

'Yes, practically. Only of course they have to be very cautious, and I suppose they can't be absolutely certain until he's quite well again.'

'But, isn't he? Well again, I mean?' Marianne felt impatient. She had been sure that today Mark would have recovered completely, would be out of the breathing apparatus, back home again.

'No, it will take a little time for him to recover. He'll have to stay in the iron lung for a bit, till all danger of infection is over, and he can't come out of hospital till he can do without the lung. And then of course he'll have a lot to make up – he won't be as far on as he was before this illness.'

[84]

'As far on in what?' Marianne asked stupidly.

'As far on in getting quite, absolutely, well again. Back to school and playing games and leading an ordinary life again. I'm afraid this means that Mark will be an invalid for quite a time to come.'

'Oh, no!' burst out of Marianne, before she had time to think.

Miss Chesterfield looked at her quickly and then said soothingly, 'Don't get upset, Marianne dear. I dare say I'm wrong about it. And anyhow so much depends on Mark himself and how much he really wants to get better quickly. He's been a bit lazy about it, you know, and perhaps having this setback will stir him up to take more interest in getting back his strength. The great thing at the moment is that he's so much better. Now, long division of pounds, shillings and pence is what we've got to get down to this morning.'

They got down to it: and Marianne was surprised, not for the first time, that one can concentrate really hard and even enjoy thinking about something which isn't at all what one is really wanting to think about. She wanted to think about supplying Mark with the things he needed in the house: but, in the meantime, comfortably secure now that he would be alive to enjoy what she was going to provide, she whipped through some tough long division of money, she wrote a few French sentences, she learnt a short poem about cowslips, she took turns with Miss Chesterfield in reading *A Tale of Two Cities* aloud, and by the end of the morning was surprised to find how quickly, and agreeably on the whole, the time had passed. *A Tale of Two Cities*, incidentally counted as three separate subjects in one. It was literature, it was history and it was reading aloud; a great saving of time, besides being interesting, Marianne thought.

So it wasn't till after her after-lunch rest or siesta, nearly tea-time, that Marianne had time to go back to her drawing book and The Pencil.

She finished the table and she drew in two chairs. She

drew a rug on the floor, and, as well as she could, a fireplace in case it was ever going to be cold in the dream. She drew a bookcase and filled it with books of every size and shape. There wasn't room to draw what the books were, but Marianne felt with satisfaction that, among so many, Mark must find several that he could read. It would be a most perverse fate that would make them all volumes of sermons or other unsuitable books. Anyhow she didn't know what sort of books he did like, but on the largest of the volumes she printed the letters R. C. for *Robinson Crusoe*.

Games were more difficult. She drew something as much like a chess-board as she could manage, with some of the pieces on it as if a game were being played; and she was careful to draw a box beside the board to hold the rest of the chessmen. She put in some draughts, because they could use the same board, but it was very difficult to draw things so tiny. She tried to draw a pack of cards, but found it impossible, so she drew a little pile of cards on the table and hoped that her thinking of them as playing cards would make them turn out to be just that.

Her best effort was the bed. She drew a four-poster, having always longed for one herself, and it rather dwarfed the room. Even the table looked small by the side of the bed, but Marianne felt that it didn't much matter, as Mark was, after all, still an invalid and would have to spend most of his time in bed. She drew several blankets and an eiderdown, pillows and sheets.

Food! Mark had mentioned that he would like some decent food. There wasn't room on the table for anything more – it was already overloaded with large chessmen, draughts and cards. So on the floor Marianne drew a dish of fruit – she had been taught a rather good way of doing this by a girl at school, and the dish of fruit was one of the best things in the picture – a cake, a loaf of bread, a string of sausages because they, too, were easy to draw realistically, and several eggs in egg-cups for the same simple reason. If you are not very good at drawing it is so easy to be too ambitious and turn out objects which are quite unrecognizable, and this was what Marianne wanted to avoid.

She had meant to end by drawing Mark, but the room was by this time so crowded there certainly wasn't room for him. She had an uncomfortable feeling that perhaps she had

filled the room with preparations for someone who wouldn't actually be there. But he was in the first picture of the room and she must rely on that and on the fact that he had always been there in her dream hitherto.

She was almost longing for bedtime, a most unusual occurrence, she was so anxious to tell Mark what she had discovered about The Pencil and to demonstrate to him the proof of its powers. And sure enough, she had hardly lain down for the night before she was asleep, and asleep was dreaming.

11. Them

The room wasn't as overcrowded in the dream as it had been in the picture: the bed took up a good deal of room, certainly, but then Marianne had meant it to be a big bed. In the big bed, leaning against the pile of pillows, was Mark. He was not looking at her, he was reading a book.

Marianne saw this, and then looked round. The other things were all there as far as she could see – bookcase full of books, table covered with games and – Marianne walked cautiously round the end of the bed and looked at the floor on the other side. There were the bread, the cake, the dish of fruit, the eggs in their egg-cups and the sausages. The sausages looked a little forlorn. One does not often see a string of fat brown sausages lying on an uncarpeted floor.

Mark was still reading. He didn't appear to have noticed Marianne's arrival, so she stood at the end of the bed and looked around, making up her mind what was still lacking in the room. It looked very much better than it had before, but it had a curious air of not quite being a complete room that anyone lived in, in spite of Mark. It looked like a box-room in which a lot of different objects have been collected which haven't much to do with each other.

Marianne took a step towards the bookcase to make sure that the books were the right sort, and trod on a floor-board that creaked. Mark looked up.

'Oh, so you're here,' he said agreeably.

'Yes.'

'It looks a bit different, doesn't it?' Mark asked, with a grin.

'Yes. Oh, Mark, are you pleased?'

'Of course I'm pleased. It's a jolly comfortable bed,' said Mark, wriggling in it slightly. 'And someone's left a lot of food about, only in a funny sort of place. I don't know if you can see it, it's on the floor.'

'I know. You see there wasn't room on the table.'

'It does seem a bit crowded,' Mark admitted. 'What's there, anyway? I saw a lot of boxes and things, but I didn't look properly.'

'There's a chess-board,' Marianne began. 'Wait a minute, I want to make sure of something.'

She opened the box beside the chess-board and looked in. There were pieces, she was glad to see. She put them out on the table and counted. With the pieces on the board there were thirty-two.

'Mark,' she said, 'how many chessmen should there be – in a whole set, I mean?'

'Thirty-two. Why? Aren't they all there?'

'Yes, they are. And it's fifty-two cards in a whole pack, isn't it?'

'Yes,' Mark said. He looked slightly surprised as Marianne began to count the pile of cards on the table. 'Why on earth are you doing that? Why shouldn't they all be there?'

'Because I couldn't draw them all separately, so I didn't know – forty-one, forty-two, forty-three – wait a minute.'

'Yes, it is a complete pack,' she announced, a moment later. 'Good. Then the draughtsmen will all be there, I expect.'

She looked, and they were.

'Look here,' said Mark impatiently, 'what is all this? Why are you so suspicious about everything not being there? Who'd have taken a chessman anyway? Why should they? It's not the sort of thing THEY want.'

'Who want?' asked Marianne, but without waiting for a reply she began to answer Mark's questions. 'Because I drew it. I drew it all, so that you'd be more comfortable. I drew the bed and the books and the table and things – only I'm not very good at drawing and I couldn't draw the things on the table small enough and so I couldn't get everything in, and I had to draw a box for the rest of the chessmen instead of drawing the whole lot, and the pack of cards and not each card, so I wanted to make sure they were all there.'

She drew breath and went on.

'And you said you wanted some decent food so I drew some. Only I had to put it on the floor because there wasn't room anywhere else, so I'm afraid it does look rather peculiar. And I drew a lot of books for you to read, but of course I couldn't draw all their names, and anyway I didn't know what sort of books you liked, so I just had to hope for the best.'

There was a short silence. Marianne felt she could not very well say any more and she was waiting for Mark's expressions of delighted gratitude.

'What do you mean you drew it?' Mark said at last.

'I drew it, just like I told you before. I draw the things and then they're here – only don't be angry, Mark, I didn't mean I'd invented you or anything, only that I can draw things and then they appear here, so I did it this time to show you it was true, because you didn't believe me.'

'You mean you drew all these things? The bed and the books and the food and everything?'

'Yes.' Marianne was still waiting for the gratitude.

'When?'

'Oh, yesterday. Today, I mean. Well, whenever it was. The day before this night, anyway.'

Mark seemed to consider this. Then he said only, 'Oh, I see.'

'Don't you believe me?' Marianne cried. She was terribly disappointed.

'Look,' said Mark; he sounded rather embarrassed. 'I'm sure you did your best, and I know you mean to be kind.

And if I believed in that sort of thing happening, I probably would believe you. But I can't. I just can't. See? It's impossible, that's all.'

'But it's true.'

'Look,' Mark said, 'I can see you think it's true, and it was nice of you to think of doing it. I'm not absolutely sure in my own mind yet, but I dare say I will be later. Anyway, I think it was jolly decent of you to bother about trying to get things for me here.'

He smiled at Marianne suddenly. It was the first time she had seen him really smile, and it made a great difference to his face.

'I want to make you more comfortable,' she said awkwardly. 'And I thought the games and things would be amusing. Would you like to play something now?'

'No, thank you,' he said. 'I don't feel like it just at the moment.'

'Would you like something to eat?'

'I'd like an apple, thanks. I say,' he added, in a quite different tone of voice, suddenly, 'how are we going to eat those sausages?'

'They're cooked already,' Marianne said, as she handed him the apple. 'That's lucky. We'll only have to warm them up.'

'How?'

Marianne looked round the room.

'Yes, I see what you mean,' she said. 'But isn't there a kitchen downstairs or something? A gas ring would do.'

'You tell me,' Mark suggested wickedly. 'You're the person who knows what's here before you've seen it, you know.'

'But I only know if I've drawn it,' Marianne said.

'And haven't you drawn a stove? Surely if you drew the sausages for me, you'd have thought of drawing something to cook on as well?'

'No, I didn't,' said Marianne flatly, not much liking being

[91]

teased. 'Isn't there anything downstairs, truly?'

'Not as far as I know,' Mark answered carelessly. He seemed to have lost interest in the subject.

'Haven't you been to see?' Marianne asked.

'No, I haven't.'

'Tell me,' Marianne said, and she knew she was risking his being angry when she asked, 'have you ever seen the rest of the house?'

Mark hesitated.

'Have you ever been out of this room?' Marianne persisted. 'You've always been here when I've seen you and you don't seem to know much about what goes on downstairs.'

'I stay here most of the time,' Mark said shortly.

'Well, when I saw two of the rooms downstairs they were empty, absolutely empty,' said Marianne. 'I'd better go and see if the back rooms have anything in them we could cook on. Or the other one next to this, though you don't often have a kitchen upstairs.'

She went to the door, but stopped with her hand on the knob.

'Of course there won't be anything there – I needn't look.' She came back to the end of the bed.

'How do you know? More magic?' Mark's voice was mocking.

Marianne knew that he was going to laugh at her. She said uncomfortably, 'There won't be anything in the rooms because I didn't draw anything there. In fact, there probably aren't any back rooms at all because I only drew the front of the house. I'm not good at perspex – whatever it is.'

Mark said nothing.

'Well?' Marianne demanded. 'Aren't you going to say anything?'

'What can I say? I've explained that I'd like to believe you if I could, and that I can't, so anything I say now is just going to sound as if I was trying to annoy you. And it was decent of you to – to get me the bed and the games and all that.'

Marianne recognized that he was really making an attempt to be friendly, and that although the gratitude she'd been so confidently expecting wasn't going to appear, she must make an effort in return.

'All right,' she said, not very graciously. 'I suppose if you really can't believe it, you can't. But soon I'll prove it to you, so you'll absolutely have to believe me.'

'That would be very nice,' Mark agreed languidly.

'For instance – tell me something you'd like here, Mark. Anything – only don't make it too difficult to draw. Then if I draw it, and it appears, you'll believe I can do it, won't you?'

'I'd like my bicycle,' Mark said promptly.

'Oh! It's not going to be easy to draw – bikes are so complicated round the pedals and chain. Besides, you couldn't ride it, could you?'

'No – o. But all the same I'd like it just to look at. It's one of the things I seem to miss most now I'm in bed such a lot and people never seem to understand that even if I can't ride it, I want it to look at.'

'Yes, I know,' Marianne said eagerly. 'All right, I'll try. I'll probably be able to draw something like a bike – I can copy Thomas's. Anything else?'

'I wish you could get me out of here,' Mark said, suddenly gloomy.

'I could try. I could draw you walking down the path away from the house, looking very pleased with yourself.'

'I told you, I can't walk.'

'But you will be able to. Perhaps if I drew you walking . . .' Marianne stopped.

'What?'

'I'd rather not say. Anyhow you wouldn't like it if I did. And I want to ask you something else. Mark?'

'What is it?'

'What did you mean when you said the chessmen weren't

the sort of thing THEY wanted? When I was counting them?'

Mark looked quickly at the window, and away again. He was suddenly wary.

'I don't want to talk about it,' he said.

'Why? I do. I want to understand. Please, Mark!'

'No. Don't be stupid.' He sounded angry.

'I don't see why it's stupid,' Marianne said. 'Why shouldn't I ask you about it, if you know and I don't? Who are THEY? Do they live here, or own the house, or what?'

'Don't talk so loud,' Mark said anxiously. 'I told you not to talk about it.'

'But why? You must tell me why?'

'It isn't safe for one thing. For goodness' sake don't shout at the top of your voice like that. I haven't discovered yet whether THEY can hear. I know they can see.'

'But who, Mark?' Marianne insisted. She, too, had dropped her voice. 'You must tell me. It might be more dangerous for me not to know, mightn't it? Anyway, now I know there is something there, hadn't you better tell me what it is?'

'It's all so vague,' Mark said.

'But frightening?'

'Well, I dare say it isn't, really. It's just not quite knowing why they are there and what they are doing. I expect if I knew all about them, I shouldn't mind them at all.'

'But who are THEY?'

'Well, they look like – you look yourself. Look between the bars, only don't let them see you. Outside the fence – you can see between the posts. Be careful.'

Marianne approached the window, keeping well to one side and peered out between the bars. Beyond the little garden was the fence of high, uneven posts. Beyond the posts she could see the outlines of squat figures, standing round the garden like sentinels. She jumped back.

'Mark! People, outside!'

'Look again,' Mark said.

Marianne peered out, more cautiously than ever. The

people stood in strangely stiff, unyielding positions. She looked fixedly at one to see him shift his position, give some indication that he was alive. But he stayed absolutely still. So did the others.

'Oh,' she cried in relief. 'They're not live people. They're only stones.'

'Be quiet,' Mark hissed at her. 'I told you, I don't know if THEY can hear as well as see.'

'See? How can stones see?'

'Look! Don't talk, look.'

Marianne looked again. It was difficult to see much of any one of the stones because of the bars and the fence hindering her view. But as she concentrated on one of the humped squat figures with all her attention, she saw suddenly a movement. A dark oval patch, which she had taken to be a hole, disappeared, as a pale eyelid dropped slowly for a moment and then was raised again. And in the dark oval, the ball of an eye swivelled slowly towards the house and remained there, staring with a fixed unwinking gaze straight, it appeared, at Marianne herself.

She shrank away from the window and turned to Mark.

'One of them looked right at me!' she said.

'I can never tell whether THEY really see me, or just pretend to,' Mark said, in a low voice.

'It's horrible!' Marianne said. She shivered suddenly. 'Mark, I'm frightened! Do they do that all the time? Don't they ever shut their eyes? Go to sleep?'

'I don't know what happens at night,' Mark said. 'I can't see them in the dark, but I have a horrible sort of feeling that they can see me.'

'Do they ever move?'

'Only their eyes. At least, I've never seen anything else move. And the same ones always seem to be in the same place every time I look out.'

'I'm frightened,' Marianne said again. 'I don't like it Mark.'

'I don't either.'

'Are THEY all round the house?'

'I don't know. I can't see at the back, of course. They're all across the front anyhow, and round as much of the sides as you can see from that window.'

'I think you're awfully brave, Mark,' Marianne said suddenly.

'Why on earth? I haven't done anything about them.'

'No. But you've been here all the time knowing about them, and you've never told me till I made you.'

'I'm not quite sure,' Mark said slowly, 'if THEY were here all the time. I somehow think they weren't, right at the beginning.'

'When did you see them first?'

'I'm not absolutely sure. I think it was when the fence got higher – the time the bars appeared, you know. I tell you what – that first time you came, before you got into the house, when you were outside the garden. Did you see them then?'

'No,' Marianne said uncomfortably.

'Well, you couldn't *not* have seen them, could you? You walked right up to the front of the house and you didn't see anything horrible – well, like THEM, did you?'

'No.'

'What's the matter?' Mark demanded. 'You've gone all queer and quiet. You needn't be so petrified. Nothing's happened to me yet, and I've been here longer than you.'

'It's not that. I am frightened, but this is something worse. Mark, don't laugh at me – but I'm feeling awful about THEM. I think it's my fault.'

'Your fault?'

'Don't be angry, Mark, and say I want to run the whole show, but I did draw some stones awfully like those out there, round the house.'

Mark was silent for a moment. Then he said, 'What about the eyes?'

'That's what's so awful. I did give them eyes.'

'What on earth did you do it for?' Mark cried out, propping himself up in bed with a sudden show of energy. 'Whatever made you draw a lot of beastly things like that if you knew what you drew was going to sort of come alive like this? Why couldn't you draw something decent for a change?'

'I'm frightfully sorry,' said Marianne, in tears. 'B-b-but I didn't know it was going to come real when I did them.'

There was a silence, broken only by a loud sniff from Marianne.

'Oh, don't cry,' said Mark, in a kinder voice. 'That won't help.'

'I'm frightfully sorry,' said Marianne again.

'All right,' Mark said. 'I know you didn't mean to do it. But it was a most asinine thing to do.'

'I know it was,' Marianne said meekly.

'And for goodness' sake don't go drawing any more horrors, will you?'

'No, of course I won't. As soon as I realized what the pencil could do, I did draw these things for you, you know. The bed and the books and the food and everything.'

'Yes, you did,' Mark agreed.

'Well, then.'

'I say,' he said suddenly, after a pause, 'couldn't you just rub them out? You said it was a pencil, didn't you? Well then, why not just get rid of them like that?'

'It's a pencil that won't rub out,' Marianne said miserably.

'Oh.'

'Then you do believe that it's the pencil that makes the things come here?' Marianne asked. 'You do think I'm telling the truth about what I draw?'

'Looks like it, doesn't it?' Mark said reluctantly.

'Perhaps I'll think of something I could do to help,' Marianne said, cheered by this admission. 'Perhaps I could make them nice instead of horrible. I'll try hard to think of what I could do.'

She went to the window and peered out again. The stone she had seen before had its open eye unceasingly on the house. Marianne jumped back.

'It is beastly, isn't it?' Mark said.

He sounded as if he needed to be reassured that she found it disturbing, too.

'I think it's horrible,' Marianne said. 'I absolutely hate it. Oh, Mark, what shall we do?'

'There's nothing we can do as far as I can see,' Mark said gloomily. 'Except wait. We can't get out, even if I could walk, with all of THEM waiting for us outside.'

'What do you think THEY would do if we tried to get out – to escape?' Marianne asked.

'I don't know,' said Mark shortly. 'I don't want to try.'

'But we must get out!' Marianne cried. 'I can't stay here for ever and nor can you. You said you had a feeling you'd got to get out. What about that, now?'

'It's still there, but I don't see what to do about it. And if it comes to that, what about your feeling of wanting to get in?'

'I don't any longer,' Marianne said, and she shivered though she was not cold. 'I wish I'd never had it. But then the outside was frightening, too – it had a horrible feel about it and I wanted to get away from it, inside somewhere. Oh, Mark, is it all beastly round here and frightening? How did we get here and why is everything outside so horrible? What are THEY watching us for? What are THEY waiting for?' Marianne's voice rose to a wail of despair.

'Shut up,' Mark said, in a vicious whisper. 'I tell you THEY can hear, I'm almost sure. Look out – careful now – and see.'

Marianne looked round the side of the window. From where she stood she could see five – six – seven of the great stones standing immovable outside. As she looked there was a movement in all of them. The great eyelids dropped; there was a moment when each figure was nothing but a hunk of stone, motionless and harmless. Then, together, the pale eyelids lifted and seven great eyeballs swivelled in their stone sockets and fixed themselves on the house.

Marianne screamed. She felt that she was screaming with the full power of her lungs, screaming like a siren: but no sound came out at all. She wanted to warn Mark, but she could not utter a word.

In her struggle she woke.

12. The Tower

When Miss Chesterfield had gone, the next day, in the brief interval before lunch, Marianne got out her drawing book and looked at her drawings of the stones round the house. Seen in flat pencil on paper they were not very alarming: they looked absurd, but not as threatening as they had appeared from Mark's window in the house. Marianne considered what she could do to make them less horrible, but nothing seemed right. She wondered whether to scribble them out with the pencil; but she had an uncomfortable feeling that if she did they would be there just the same under the scribble. And it would be no better if they were really there just the same, and if she and Mark were unable to see them. She thought of adding mouths, noses and hair to the eyes, to make them more human; she tried this experimentally with an ordinary pencil, one which she knew she could rub out. The effect was grotesque and somehow more horrible. Marianne decided that though the stones with eyes were bad enough, the stones with faces were worse, and she rubbed them out vigorously, thankful that she hadn't drawn them with The Pencil first.

All that day, and all the next, Marianne considered the problem: but no answer presented itself. Meanwhile she slept without dreaming, which was a relief, although she felt guiltily that perhaps she ought to have managed to get back to Mark in the lonely little house to cheer him up, even if she couldn't see how to set him free.

'But is he there now?' she wondered. 'After all, I'm there when I'm dreaming, but I'm here when I'm awake. I suppose

Mark is awake now, so he's here in this life. And perhaps I really don't need to go back, because after all it is only a dream, and the real Mark isn't in a house with beastly Things all round it, he's safe here.'

But this reminded her that the real Mark wasn't so very safe. He was in hospital, in an iron lung, being watched by nurses and doctors and his parents for signs of getting better: or worse.

'But I can't do anything about that,' Marianne protested to herself. 'It isn't my fault he's in hospital, it's because he caught a cold, Miss Chesterfield said so. And nothing I can do now can possibly make any difference to how he gets on there. And anyway I can't think of anything to prevent those beastly stones being there or watching the house all the time. So I'm not going to bother about it. Dr Burton said it was bad for me to worry, so I won't.'

So Marianne shut up The Pencil with the other ordinary pencils, and put the drawing book under a pile of other, less disturbing books and concentrated on not worrying. This is not an easy thing to do: and whether she was sewing her patchwork, or listening to her mother reading aloud, or reading herself, or working with Miss Chesterfield, Marianne had at the back of her mind an uneasy niggle of a thought, that there was something she ought to be thinking about and wasn't.

Other people noticed it in different ways.

'Yes, she's getting on,' Dr Burton said to her mother, after one of his twice-weekly visits. 'Of course it's slow, very slow. It may be more than six weeks in bed at this rate, but still she's young and she's plenty of time, and we know that it's only a matter of time till she's absolutely right again. I'm going to change her medicine again today and see if we can give her a bit more of a will to get better.'

'Getting on quite all right,' was Miss Chesterfield's report to Marianne's mother. 'I don't know if she has got a little bored with being all alone in her work, or whether it's that she's feeling the strain of being in bed for so long: but she's not getting on quite as quickly as she did at the beginning. I think she finds it difficult to concentrate sometimes.'

'Yes, she's bored all right,' said Marianne's mother to Marianne's father. 'Something seems to have gone wrong for the last week or so. At first she was getting on so well, and seemed to have settled down quite contentedly to the routine of being an invalid. But just lately she's been irritable and difficult to amuse and restless, as if she was worrying about something. And if I ask her if there's anything wrong she always says no, there isn't.'

'No, of course, there's nothing wrong,' said Marianne disagreeably the next day, when Miss Chesterfield asked her the same question. 'I'm not worried about anything. Why on earth should I be worried? And I wish you wouldn't keep on asking me when I've said I'm perfectly all right twenty times already.'

'I'm sorry,' said Miss Chesterfield peaceably. 'I didn't realize you'd been asked before. But you know, Marianne, you aren't working as well as you were a short time ago, and I know perfectly well it isn't because you can't, so I thought perhaps you were bothered about something.'

'I haven't got anything to bother about,' Marianne said sulkily.

'Well, I'm very glad to hear it. Now turn to page 118 and we'll –'

'What did you think I might be worried about?' Marianne interrupted.

'I suppose anyone who has to stay in bed might worry about how long they'd got to stay there,' Miss Chesterfield said reasonably. 'Or I thought perhaps you were worried about Mark again. I noticed you hadn't asked about him and I wondered if you were frightened to.'

'Why should I be frightened?' Marianne asked quickly.

'In case he was worse. But he isn't, it's quite all right.'

'Is he better?' Marianne demanded. It was somehow an

enormous relief to be talking about the real Mark: almost as much as to have been helping the Mark in the dream.

'Yes, a little. He's holding his own quite well and they think that if he goes on as he is now, he'll be able to come out of the lung in a week or two.'

'Do you mean he's still in that beastly machine?' Marianne asked, sitting bolt upright in bed in surprise.

'Yes, of course. He's never come out of it since he started being ill. But he's very good about it – his mother says he never complains.'

'No, Mark doesn't complain.' Marianne remembered how it had been she who had told him how uncomfortable the window seat and the bare room were. Mark had been angry sometimes, and sometimes irritating, but never complaining.

'You sound as if you knew him,' Miss Chesterfield said, surprised by Marianne's statement.

'I almost feel as if I do from your talking about him,' Marianne said carefully. 'But why is it so awfully slow, Miss Chesterfield? I thought he wasn't going to have to stay in hospital so very long – after all, he only had a cold.'

'With bronchitis. That's what made it such a long business,' Miss Chesterfield said.

'And is he getting better as quickly as he could?' Marianne persisted.

'I'm not quite sure. His mother says he seems rather depressed, and she can't make out whether that is because he's not getting better as quickly as they'd hoped, or whether he's being slow getting better because he's depressed.'

Marianne did not ask any more questions. Part of her mind now told her that she ought to be satisfied about Mark, who was, after all, doing quite well and was safe in hospital. But another part, a niggling, tiresome part that wouldn't quite keep quiet, told her that Mark was alone in a house watched all round by THEM, and that she had left him there and had never even tried to help.

'He's perfectly all right,' most of Marianne said to the

rest of Marianne. 'There's nothing for you to bother yourself about. All that business about the house and THEM is just a dream.'

'But he was there in my dream,' the small persistent part of Marianne said. 'And I said I'd help him and I didn't. I left him there more than a week ago with all those eyes looking at the house.'

'It doesn't matter what you do in dreams,' the sensible, comforting voice said. 'They don't count for real life.'

'They are real themselves,' said the other voice: and Marianne knew it was true. 'How you behave in a dream is just as real as how you behave when you are awake.'

'Oh dear,' said the whole of Marianne miserably. 'I shall have to go back into the house and I don't want to. I don't want to.'

She got out her drawing book from under the pile later in the day and looked at what she had done again. She could still see no way of making the stone figures less terrifying. She could, however, give Mark his bicycle, she thought, and she decided to put it in one of the empty downstairs rooms. She was very uncertain exactly what a bicycle looked like, but, 'After all,' she thought, 'when I drew Mark it wasn't

any more like a real boy than my pictures generally are, and he came out looking quite ordinary.'

So with The Pencil, she drew something with two wheels and handlebars and a saddle, standing proudly by itself in a downstairs room. Pump, chain, and brakes Marianne wisely left to the imagination, and when she had finished, it really did look like a real bicycle.

'What else might we need?' she thought. 'Food. Mark must have almost finished the food I drew before. There wasn't very much. And I must put in lights somehow for when it gets dark.'

She drew electric lights hanging from the ceiling of each room and in the hall; and then in case they might not work without her drawing the means by which electricity came into the house, a task quite beyond her, she also drew a candlestick and candle on the floor beside the bicycle. She was proud of herself for remembering to add a box of matches. She added some more eggs in egg-cups and what she hoped looked like a roast chicken on a plate.

'He's got enough books,' she thought, looking at the drawing of the bookcase, which was indeed as full of books as she could make it. 'And chess, and draughts, and cards. I can't think of anything else.'

She turned her attention again to the outside of the house. The hills in the distance looked bare. Marianne added tiny trees and a sort of thick pencil fuzz for bushes at the foot of one or two of them. On the top of the highest hill she drew a tower, round and squat, with battlements on top. She had had no idea of what sort of building it would be, but when it was finished it reminded her of a stubby lighthouse. She put slit windows up the walls and an extra dome-shaped top above the battlements, where there could be the light.

'It shines out to sea,' she said to herself. 'Everyone can see it for miles around.'

Somehow it was a comforting thought that the sea was the other side of the hills. She had forgotten that when she had been concentrating on the house and its immediate surroundings. The house, and the stunted garden, were hemmed in, too cramped and small: and the evil, watching stones made it seem even more of a prison. But to know that not far away, along the road and beyond the hills was the sea, free and salt and without bounds, was like having prison gates opened, even if it was not yet time to go out.

'I'll tell Mark,' Marianne thought. 'I know he'll be pleased. Perhaps he knows already. I'll tell him about the sea.'

She had no doubts that she would be with him again that night, her thoughts had been so much with her drawings. So it was no surprise, after she had gone to sleep, to find herself standing at the bottom of the stairs in the nearly empty house, listening to the tick of the clock on the landing upstairs. It was not very light, about dusk, Marianne judged, and in case it became too dark to see her way about, she turned first into the room on her right. There, to her immense satisfaction, was the bicycle, oddly surrounded on the floor by egg-cups, a candlestick and a roast chicken.

She walked round the bicycle several times, admiring its shiny black and silver newness and its completeness of equipment with the pride of a creator. If she had put it together herself, piece by piece, instead of having only drawn it, she could hardly have been more pleased.

Having satisfied herself that it had everything a bicycle ought to have, she picked up the candlestick and the roast chicken and went upstairs. To her knock on Mark's door, an impatient voice called, 'Come in.'

He was still in bed, still propped rather listlessly on pillows. He had put down the book he had been reading and was looking at her with an expression she could not fathom. Marianne remembered, with shame now, how she had screamed when the stone eyes turned towards her, how she had run away and left Mark alone. 'Not that I can help waking up, at least I don't think I can,' she thought. 'But then I didn't try to come back to see how he was or what was happening.'

She had meant to greet Mark with the news of his bicycle downstairs: she was longing to hear his grateful thanks. To her surprise she said what she hadn't meant to, or even thought of. 'I'm sorry, Mark.'

'It's all right,' he said, sounding embarrassed. 'You didn't do anything.'

'I didn't come back.'

'Well, I suppose you couldn't.'

'Yes, I think I could. And you aren't any better. Oh, Mark, I am so sorry. Do say you forgive me.'

'Oh, don't fuss,' was Mark's answer. 'You're back now, aren't you? Don't get so excited.' Suddenly he laughed, unexpectedly. 'If you only knew how funny you look, standing there saying, "do forgive me", with a candlestick in one hand and that great plate in the other. What on earth is it? A duck, or something?'

'It's roast chicken,' Marianne said eagerly. 'I thought you might be hungry.'

'Jolly good idea. I am a bit hungry. The trouble is I got a bit sick of eggs and sausages. The fruit was jolly good, though.'

'But you can't have been eating eggs and sausages ever since I was here last,' Marianne said, surprised.

'I have, though. Why not?'

'I didn't think I'd drawn enough.'

'There always seems to be some more, however much I eat,' Mark said indifferently. 'Look round this side of the bed and you'll see. Put the chicken down, silly, you can't carry it about in one hand all the time.'

Marianne put the chicken on the floor – the table was still overloaded – and came round to the window side of the room. The floor was indeed still covered with eggs, and the string of sausages was also still there. Near the bed was a neat pile of empty eggshells.

[107]

'I say, you've eaten quite a lot,' Marianne exclaimed. 'But I'm sure there are just as many as I drew at first. Why do you keep the shells there?'

'No waste-paper basket. One of the things you forgot when you furnished this room,' Mark said, grinning.

'Why didn't you throw them out of the window?'

Mark only looked at her for reply. The look reminded Marianne for the first time of what was outside the windows.

'Are THEY still there?' she asked, in a low voice. 'Are they still watching?'

'I haven't looked lately,' Mark answered in the same tone. 'Last time I did, they were.'

'All of them?'

'Yes, all of them.'

'Let's eat the chicken,' Marianne said abruptly. She picked up the dish and put it on the end of the four-poster bed.

'Where are the plates?' she asked, looking round.

'You tell me,' Mark said.

'Oh! I didn't draw any! Oh, I am stupid! Nor knives or forks or anything. I am so sorry, Mark! What shall we do?'

'Stop apologizing and eat with our fingers. I've done it before on picnics, and I've been eating the sausages without anything like that all this time. Give me the cockatoo – I'll carve.'

He did, with great dexterity, separating the chicken into neat manageable joints. Marianne found she was hungry; hungrier than Mark, in fact, who, in spite of having admittedly got tired of sausages and eggs, ate very little, and before Marianne had finished was leaning back on his pillows, watching her.

'This is the only way to eat a chicken,' Marianne said, cleaning up a drumstick in a most satisfactory way. 'I never can get all the bits off with a knife and fork. Aren't you going to eat any more?'

'No.'

'You didn't eat very much.'

'I'm not hungry.'

'You said you were.'

'Well, I thought I was, but when I start eating I'm not. Not as much as I expected.'

'Wouldn't you like something else? A banana or something?'

'What else is there?' Mark asked lazily.

'Well, I don't think there is anything else. You see I didn't realize that the food you ate didn't sort of get used up so I'm afraid I drew some more eggs.'

'More eggs? Where are they? I don't see them.'

'They're downstairs. Oh, Mark! I'd forgotten! Your bicycle.'

'What about it?'

'It's here. It's downstairs. I drew it and it's here, like the other things.'

Mark lost all his appearance of indifference. He sat bolt upright in bed and looked really animated.

'Well, I must say, that's jolly decent of you,' he said. 'One of the things I really wanted was my bike.'

'One of the things? What else do you want?'

'Oh, nothing you can draw. Just to be able to walk again. That's all. Tell me about the bike. What colour is it?'

'Black. And silver. And I think it's got all its bits, Mark. I looked very carefully.'

'All its bits?'

'Well, all the things like brakes and chains and the little wheels that make it work. I couldn't draw it very well, but it's come out all right.'

'Does it go? That's the thing,' Mark said.

'I didn't try. I'll go down and see – only it's getting awfully dark.'

'It doesn't matter,' Mark said, throwing himself back on his pillows. 'It won't make any difference. I shan't be able to ride it anyhow.'

'But, Mark, you will!'

'Not for ages. Perhaps not ever.'

He shut his eyes. Marianne did not speak. When he opened them again and saw her face, he said quickly, 'But it was jolly decent of you to get it for me. Thanks.'

'It's almost dark,' Marianne said, hoping to cheer him up. 'Let's see if the lights work. Did you notice we've got electric light now?'

She went towards the switch, but before she could turn it on, Mark cried out, 'No!' so suddenly that she jumped.

'Why not? Anyway, they may not work. That's why I brought the candle.'

'Don't! We don't want a light on! You're not to, Marianne! Leave the light alone!'

'But why?' Marianne demanded. 'What harm can it possibly do us?'

'Don't be stupid,' Mark said fiercely. 'Use your brains if you've got any. Think what's outside. If we have a light on in here, THEY can see right in, can't they? And see how many of us there are, and that I can't walk and know everything about us. Is that what you want?'

Marianne stood quite still: only her hand, which had been raised to the light switch, fell to her side again. She was suddenly cold. Beyond the barred window the sky was a deepening grey. Inside the room it was very dark indeed.

13. The Light

'Couldn't we even have the candle?' Marianne said at last, in a small voice. 'It would only be a very little light.'

'I think we'd better not –' Mark began: but he broke off and cried out, 'What's that?'

For the whole room was suddenly lit up by a glow of yellowish light. A great beam swept slowly past the window. It was followed by a darkness which seemed the blacker because the light had been so bright.

'Mark?' Marianne said, questioning.

'I don't know.'

'Has it ever happened before?'

'Never when I've been here.'

'It came just when you said we shouldn't have a light in here, in case THEY should see in.'

'I know. I don't like it.'

'Do you think THEY put it on? Do you think THEY heard what we said and did it on purpose?'

'They might,' Mark said. He spoke very quietly now. 'It would be just like them.'

'How do you know? Do you really know what would be like them and what wouldn't?'

'I don't know anything,' Mark said emphatically, but still low. 'Except that they watch us all the time and they're beastly. They want to hurt us somehow and they're trying all the time to do it. That's why –'

He broke off. Another great shaft of light swept past the room again, from right to left as before. When it went this time it left the room in total darkness.

'THEY are doing it again,' Marianne breathed. She moved over towards the bed to have the comfort of Mark's nearness.

'We don't know that it is THEM,' Mark whispered back.

'It must be. THEY are looking in, like you said they would and seeing how to kill us or do something horrible to us,' Marianne said in terror. 'Next time probably they'll all be waiting to come in and get us.'

She took another step towards the bed and groped for something to hold on to. She found it. It was a thin arm in a pyjama sleeve. To her surprise Mark did not immediately brush her off.

'I don't think we can be certain that it is THEM,' he said, in a voice that only trembled slightly.

'Why? Who else could it possibly be?'

'Well, it's the kind of light that puzzles me,' Mark said, still whispering, but gaining confidence as he spoke. 'It reminds me of something, but I can't quite remember what. Only it doesn't seem to me the sort of light anyone would use if they wanted to see in from outside.'

'Why not?'

'It's too quick for one thing. I'd expect it to come right in and stop and go over things, like your eyes would if you were looking about. Oh!'

As he finished his sentence the light came again. Marianne shut her eyes. She didn't want to see stone faces pressed against the window, stone eyes staring in. She felt Mark's arm shake slightly, then she saw through her closed lids that the darkness had returned and she opened her eyes again.

'Nothing came in?'

'No.' Mark's voice was not shaking at all now. 'And I've thought of what the light is like. It's like a searchlight. And I don't believe THEY would use a searchlight to look at us with. It wouldn't be enough use.'

'THEY could be trying it out, ready to turn it on this house when they've found the right place,' Marianne suggested. 'And then –'

'There's another thing,' Mark interrupted her. 'It comes now and then, not all the time like searchlights looking for something. It's more like – oh, what is it that looks like a searchlight but comes regularly, with so many minutes between each? I know. Of course. It's the light from a lighthouse.'

Marianne suddenly saw. She gasped – but as the light came round again she did not shut her eyes or flinch. She shook Mark's arm vigorously in her excitement.

'Mark, you're right, you're absolutely right. I'd forgotten, and anyhow I never thought of it actually working, when I drew it and it looked like a lighthouse, but of course that's what it is. It isn't THEM! I am so glad! I am so glad!'

This time Mark did free his arm from her grasp rather abruptly.

'Marianne, do for goodness' sake explain properly,' he said, exasperated. 'I know you think it's as clear as daylight, but it isn't. It's just an awful muddle. Start at the beginning about what you'd forgotten and tell me what I'm absolutely right about.'

'The lighthouse! The light! It does come from a lighthouse!

[113]

I drew one on top of the hills behind the house. I only put it in today, so of course it never shone before. And I didn't realize till I'd drawn it what it was. It began by being just a building on a hill. But it is a lighthouse, and its working, so it isn't THEM, it's us!'

'What do you mean, it's us? Why shouldn't THEY be there, too?'

'I don't know,' Marianne began. She stopped as the great beam of light swung past the windows again, and then went on. 'I suppose it's only a feeling, but sometimes what you feel is just as real as what you know, and I've got that sort of feeling now that the lighthouse is on our side, not on theirs.'

'I've always liked lighthouses,' Mark admitted.

'And, anyway, if it's THEM, why didn't they turn the light right in on us like you said?'

'I should think you're right,' Mark said slowly. 'Only I wish we were sure it was your lighthouse. Couldn't you look and see?'

'Go right up to the window?'

'Yes. Carefully so THEY can't see you.'

Marianne hesitated. She did not at all want to go to the window to see the watchers outside, but she also did not want to say she would not go. Mark watched her from the bed.

'I know it comes from the lighthouse. It couldn't come from anywhere else.'

'You can't be absolutely sure till you've seen it.'

'You don't believe me.'

'I'll believe you when you've actually seen it come from the lighthouse.'

While Marianne still hesitated, the beam went past the window again. In the darkness that followed she summoned all her courage and said, 'All right. I will.'

She felt her way round the end of the bed. The window was a pale oblong crossed by dark bars and she moved cautiously towards it, knocking over more than one egg-cup on her way.

'Hi!' said Mark's voice teasing, but encouraging, from the bed, 'don't kick the eggs about too much.'

Marianne felt for the window seat and found it. She slid her hand up the side of the window frame and established herself to one side of the window where she could look out without being seen.

'Marianne? Have you got there?'

'Yes. I'm waiting for the light.'

'See if you can see where it comes from. Oh!' His voice changed. 'I am a fool. Of course you won't be able to.'

'Why?' asked Marianne. But as she spoke the shaft of light came round, flooding the country outside. In that moment Marianne saw the bleak tussocky grass stretching far away, the tall fence and the little garden, like a picture flashed for a moment on a screen and then gone. But in that moment she had seen something else, an impression she could hardly be sure of after so quick a glance.

'I can't see where it comes from, it goes too fast,' she said. 'And it goes past the house as if it came from somewhere behind us.'

'Yes, of course. That's what I was going to say. Of course you won't be able to see where it comes from, because if you could the light would shine right into the room. It must be coming from somewhere that you can't see from the window.'

'Then it is the lighthouse,' Marianne said, turning towards the bed, though she could see nothing in the dark room. 'Because the lighthouse is on the hills and the hills are behind the house. That's the way I drew them.'

'Did you draw anything else?'

'Not outside. Only inside. Your bicycle and the chicken.'

'And all those eggs,' Mark said. The eggs had somehow become a very good joke. 'I wish I could see the bike, though. I've always wanted one of my own.'

'Can you ride?' Marianne asked.

'Yes. A friend of mine has one and I ride his. At least I used to.'

'Wait a moment,' Marianne said. She had seen the shaft of light approaching again. It swept round and she looked out cautiously and saw the same scene as before: but this time she concentrated on one thing only.

The light passed and she saw it. What she had only suspected before she was now certain of.

'Mark, I must tell you. THEY don't like the light.'

'How do you know?'

'When it comes round they shut their eyes. And they look somehow as if they were huddling together.'

'But they can't move.'

'I know, but still that is how they look. Much more than in the daytime.'

'How do you know they only shut their eyes when the light comes? They may sleep all night.'

'I suppose they might,' Marianne said doubtfully. 'I hadn't thought of that. I'll look again and see if I can see them actually shutting their eyes. Didn't you say THEY could see in the dark?'

'I said I thought they could. But, of course, I couldn't ever see. I just had a feeling they were watching me all the time.'

'Perhaps they don't like any kind of light. What happens when the sun shines here?'

'I don't know.' Mark's voice sounded doubtful. 'The sun has never shone when I've been here.'

Marianne tried to think if she'd seen sunshine there, but all she could remember was the chill half-light in which she had first seen the house and which seemed to have persisted ever since. She remained standing by the window, waiting for the first sign of the lighthouse's beam: but this time, feeling braver, and anxious to see what happened outside as soon as possible, she stood in the centre of the window and looked for the beam.

She saw it, this time, coming from the right, far away, a great golden shaft of light, crossing what looked like miles of grassy plain. As it first struck the fence round the house Marianne saw, distinctly with no possibility of doubt, a flinching stone eye shut. Not the slow dropping of the lid she had seen before, but a quicker recoil from a brightness intolerable to the cold dark eyeball beneath. She looked quickly to the other side, but those petrified eye-lids remained immovable while the light was still on them.

'I saw one,' she said, as the darkness succeeded the light. 'And THEY do shut their eyes when the light comes, Mark. First it was open and then it shut, and it shut as if it didn't like the light.'

Mark did not answer.

'Mark!'

'I heard you the first time,' Mark said. 'But I didn't see what there was to say.'

'Well, doesn't it show that the light and the lighthouse are their enemies? That they're on our side?'

'I suppose so. But I don't see how that's going to help us much. What can a lighthouse, on a hill, miles away, do to help us get out of here? THEY are much nearer. And anyhow, why a lighthouse? What use is a lighthouse in the middle of the land?'

'It isn't,' said Marianne indignantly. 'I'm not as stupid as that. On the other side of the hills is the sea.'

'The sea!' Marianne could hear that Mark had moved suddenly in bed as if the words had stirred him. 'Are you sure?'

'Quite sure.'

'So it's not very far away?'

'Not very. I don't know how far the hills are from here – about a mile or two, I should think; and the sea must be just the other side of them.'

Mark said nothing.

'Do you like the sea?' Marianne asked.

[117]

'Yes.'

'Mark, let's go to the sea!'

'I wish we could,' Mark said, in a voice that was almost a groan.

'We can. It's not very far. Do let's try.'

'My good girl,' said Mark, in a tone of exaggerated patience. 'Aren't you forgetting the fact that I can't move out of this bed except on all fours? Even if the sea was half a mile away, I couldn't possibly get there.'

There was a pause. Then Marianne said, 'I'm sorry.'

'All right, but it's no good. Don't go on about it, because I couldn't do it.'

After a moment's silence he added, 'I tell you what. You go!'

'No,' said Marianne, before she knew she was going to speak, and very emphatically. 'I won't go without you. I shan't go unless you can come too.'

'Well, then, you won't go, because I can't. And anyhow I don't see how you'd get out of the house. What about THEM?'

'I'd get out,' Marianne said, visited by an inspiration, 'while THEY had their eyes shut when the light came round.'

Mark seemed to be considering this. Then he said grudgingly, 'Yes, I suppose you could. It would be risky. You'd have to get out very quickly.'

'Well, I could.'

'You go then,' Mark urged. 'Why on earth should you wait here just because I can't get out? You don't have to look after me, you know. I'm perfectly all right by myself.'

'Are you quite certain you couldn't walk?' Marianne asked hesitantly.

'Of course I am. I told you.'

'Oughtn't you to practise a bit? I mean will your legs get any better if you don't try to use them?'

'I don't know,' Mark said shortly, 'I wish you wouldn't go on about it. I've told you I can't go and that's flat.'

'Well, I'm not going till you can come,' Marianne began, but she broke off and said suddenly, 'I know! Your bicycle!'

'What about my bike?'

'You could ride it. Mark, you could! Then the way to the sea wouldn't seem so long. Do let's try.'

Mark's voice sounded thoughtful when he spoke again, but there was an undercurrent of excitement. 'I wonder if I could.'

'I'm sure you could.'

'I don't know. You see it's the muscles of my legs, they say, that aren't any good. I don't know if I could turn the pedals.'

'Let's try,' Marianne pleaded.

'Now, in the dark? Really, Marianne, sometimes you are a complete idiot.'

'I know,' said Marianne, undismayed. 'But I get excited when I think of something and I want to do it now. Don't you?'

'Sometimes. But not this time. It's too dark. Only, just tell me where the bike is.'

'Downstairs. In the room on the left as you come down.'

'Thanks.'

There was a long silence. The light outside passed five or six times before Marianne said, 'Mark?'

A very sleepy voice answered, 'What is it?'

'Will you try, then?'

'Might,' said the voice. 'Not now. Another day. Got to go to sleep now. Can't talk any . . .'

His words slurred off into a long breath. Marianne gave a sympathetic yawn, felt her own eyelids heavy, her thoughts confused. Leaning her head against the window frame she fell deeply asleep.

And woke.

14. The Bicycle

'Well, young woman,' Dr Burton said, putting his stetho-
scope away and shutting his case with a snap. 'You're getting
on very well. Very well indeed. It won't be long now before
we have you up and about again.'

'Get up?' said Marianne. She gave a preliminary bounce
in bed. 'When? Now? Today?'

'My word, you're in a hurry. No, not today nor tomorrow.
Not for a week or so, and then when you do get up you'll
have to go very slowly.'

'Not for a week!' Marianne exclaimed in dismay.

'Not for more than a week. After all you've been two
months or more in bed already; you can put up with another
few days!'

'I thought you meant I could get up at once.'

'No. I said you were doing very well, and it may be sooner
than we thought at the time, that's all. But we mustn't rush
things, just because you are getting better. We want to get
you quite well so that you can forget you ever had an illness
at all and don't have to be careful not to do all the things
you want to: running, bicycling and so on.'

'Oh!' Marianne said, 'I've just remembered, I wanted to
ask you something.'

'Go ahead.'

'If someone – if I hadn't had the illness I did have, but
that other one where you can't walk properly afterwards
because your muscles don't work –'

'Polio, do you mean?'

'I don't know its name. I know people who have it have

to go into a sort of breathing machine to make their lungs work properly.'

'Yes, that's polio,' Dr Burton said. 'Well, go on. If you'd had that, what?'

'Would I be able to bicycle?'

'That depends on how badly the muscles of your legs were affected.'

'If I couldn't walk, but I could crawl?'

'What is this?' Dr Burton demanded. 'A test of my medical knowledge? Or are you writing a textbook on disease? None of this has anything to do with what happened to you.'

'I'm not writing anything,' Marianne said. 'I just wondered. I heard of someone who'd had that polio thing and who wanted a bicycle, so I was thinking about whether they'd be able to ride it.'

'Best thing she could do if she's strong enough,' Dr Burton said briskly, picking up his case and going towards the door. 'They often use bicycles, stationary of course, in hospitals for getting power back into wasted muscles. Tell your friend to hop on her bicycle and pedal for dear life. If her doctor agrees, of course. Good-bye. See you next week. Stay put till then, now, no jumping out of bed and bicycling for you just yet.'

'So it wouldn't hurt Mark to bicycle,' Marianne thought with satisfaction. 'I do hope he'll try next time I'm there.'

Later in the day she took out her drawing book and, turning to the original picture of the inside of the house, she added a little Mark on the stairs. She meant to draw him stepping down, but owing to the difficulty of making legs look as if they were walking, she found that in fact she had made him sit rather more than half-way down the staircase. To the bicycle she added what was meant to be a stand to keep it upright while Mark practised on it. This room now had no space left for any more drawings, so in the empty room, on the opposite side of the hall, Marianne drew a tin on the outside of which she carefully printed in tiny letters, 'TOFFEE'.

'Now,' she thought, 'if I can get back there when it's light, I'll get Mark to practise on the bicycle.'

It was light, and she was in the room downstairs when she found herself back in the dream that night. She was alone with the tin of toffee. Before she went up to see Mark, she looked quickly into the opposite room and saw the bicycle firmly anchored on what looked like a very solid stand.

She had half expected to see Mark as she had drawn him, on the stairs, but the staircase was empty as she went up. Only the clock ticked steadily over the door to Mark's room.

'The clock is friendly, too,' Marianne thought for the first time. 'I'm glad of the clock. It comforts me, like the light-house.'

Mark was sitting up in bed reading. He looked up, said, briefly but agreeably, 'Hullo,' and dropped his eyes back to the book.

'Have a toffee?' Marianne said, seating herself on the end of his bed.

'Thanks.' He waited while she opened the lid of the tin, and helped himself as she held it towards him. 'Did you draw that too?'

'Yes. Downstairs. I've just brought it up.'

'Good idea.' His eyes dropped to his book.

'Don't you ever do anything except read?' Marianne exclaimed.

'Not much. Nothing else to do. Besides I like reading,' Mark murmured without looking up.

Marianne was silent from sheer exasperation. Mark went on, in the same deliberately casual voice, 'By the way, I've seen the bike. It's jolly fine.'

'You've seen it! You mean you've been downstairs?'

'Well, the bike doesn't seem to be up here, does it? Looks as if I must have been down.'

'Oh, Mark, that's marvellous! Was it –' she hesitated. 'Did you find it difficult?'

'It wasn't awfully easy,' he said uncomfortably. He stopped, and then seemed to take courage. 'I did it sitting down. It's better that way.'

'Oh, of course –' Marianne began, but she did not finish. 'Did you try the bicycle?' she asked.

'No. I couldn't get on.'

'Doesn't the stand hold it steady? I made it specially thick so that it would.'

'It wasn't that. I expect it does. I can't get up to the saddle, that's the trouble,' Mark said, with difficulty.

'I'll get you up,' Marianne said. 'I'm sure I could. Do try again, now.'

'Not now. I'm reading.'

'You're not. I've interrupted you and you've stopped for the moment. Do come and try while I'm here to help.'

'It takes such ages.'

'I don't mind. Please, Mark. I won't look if you mind my seeing you going downstairs.'

'There's nothing to look at,' Mark said. 'Only I hate it. I hate not being able just to get up and walk down like an ordinary person. I feel such a fool letting myself down the stairs like a baby.'

'It must be horrible,' Marianne said sympathetically.

'And it's partly the not knowing. Not knowing if I'll ever be all right again, or if I'm always going to be like this.'

'But you will be all right! You must be! And bicycling's the best thing you could do to make your muscles strong again.'

'Who said so?' Mark asked suspiciously.

'Dr Burton. He's our doctor. He comes to see me twice a week. I asked him about bicycling for people who've had your illness, and he said it was what they do in hospitals to get the muscles working again. On a stationary bicycle of course, but the one downstairs is.'

'How do the people in hospital get on the bicycles?'

'I suppose they have to be helped on. Oh, please, Mark,

do try. We could get away from here, you know, if you could bicycle. If people in hospitals can do it, why shouldn't we?'

'All right,' Mark said. 'We'll try,' He didn't sound very hopeful. He pushed the bedclothes back and moved awkwardly towards the edge of the bed. Marianne watched him anxiously. He hesitated, and looked at her, flushing painfully.

'I can't walk, you know,' he said. 'I have to sort of drag myself. It's beastly.'

'I know,' Marianne said gently.

'Here goes,' Mark said, with a crooked smile at her. He slipped over the side of the bed and let himself down to a sitting position on the floor.

'You go first,' he said. 'Open the door for me, will you? I'll come down after you.'

Marianne opened the door and went out, without looking back, which was what she knew Mark wanted. She went downstairs and waited. She heard Mark shuffle along the floor to the doorway of his room and begin a painful descent of the stairs. He sat on one step, put his left leg on to the step below and then with his hands let his body and his right leg down to the lower step. It took a long time and when he had reached the bottom step but one, he paused, breathless. He saw Marianne looking at him, and scowled.

She said at once, boldly, 'Mark, isn't one of your legs stronger than the other?'

'I don't know. They both feel like cotton-wool. As if they didn't belong to me, but if I do anything at all, they ache. I'm sick of it.'

'But I do think one of them – that one, the left – is better than the other.'

'Why?'

'It's the one you always put down the step first, so I think it must feel stronger.'

'Perhaps you're right,' Mark said in a less unfriendly voice. He felt the leg with his hand. 'Let's go and have a look at the bike. You go first and open the door.'

Marianne went, and waited by the stationary bicycle till Mark had made his way to her. She gave it a little shake to see if it were steady, and thought it was certainly firm enough to take Mark's light weight.

'Now,' said Mark, from the floor beside her. 'Do you think you can get me up?'

'Catch hold of me and the bicycle. It's quite steady enough. Now you pull, and I'll pull. I'm sure I'll get you up.'

It was more difficult than Marianne had expected. Mark was surprisingly heavy and she had not realized that when he was pulled up to her own level his legs would take no weight at all, and she and the bicycle would have to support

him entirely. Scarlet in the face, clutching Mark's flesh unmercifully through his pyjama jacket, she hauled and pushed and strained, and behold, at last, he was in the saddle!

'You'll have to put my feet on the pedals,' Mark said, in a matter-of-fact voice. 'I can't.'

Marianne did.

'Now, pedal!' she said.

Mark shook his head.

'I can't! My legs won't do it.'

'Try!'

'I am trying. Nothing happens, that's all!' Mark said furiously.

'I'll push, too, with my hand,' Marianne said.

She tried, but as Mark had said, nothing happened. The pedals were stuck.

'It's the bicycle. It isn't you, anyway,' Marianne said. 'They just won't go round. I'll try turning them backwards.'

The pedals went round backwards with no difficulty at all and Mark's feet with them.

'That feels jolly queer,' he said. 'You're doing all the work and my legs just go round without my doing anything.'

'Try. See if you can do it by yourself.'

After a moment's hesitation, Mark tried – Marianne saw him frown as he concentrated on the task, and she frowned herself with anxiety as she watched the pedals. At first nothing happened: they remained still. Then, very slowly, Mark's left foot pushed its pedal down a very little, then a little more, then right down to the bottom. It stopped, and Mark looked at Marianne.

'I did it,' he said.

'Good. Can you do the other?'

He tried, but though the pedal moved slightly, it did not go down.

'Then your left leg is better than your right one,' Marianne said practically. 'But if you practise, the right one will get better, too. I saw the pedal move a bit, it's just not as strong. Look, I'll move this one down with my hand, and you push that left one with your foot.'

This manoeuvre worked well, and Mark with growing

confidence pushed hard enough to make the pedals revolve so fast that Marianne had no work to do.

'If you could fasten my left foot on to the pedal somehow, I could do it all by myself,' Mark said. 'We need one of those metal toe-pieces racing bicycles have on their pedals.'

'I could tie a piece of string round to hold your foot in,' Marianne suggested.

'Have you got a piece of string?'

'No. But I could use my handkerchief. Oh, bother, I haven't got one.'

'Never mind,' Mark said. 'Don't bother now. I don't think I'll do any more just at the moment.'

Marianne realized that for someone who had been in bed for so long, the effort of getting downstairs and on to the bicycle had been prodigious. She said gently, 'I'll help you off.'

'Thanks,' Mark said, when he was on the ground again. He looked closely at the bicycle and said, 'It looks all right. I wonder why the pedals only go round backwards?'

'Perhaps the brakes are on?' Marianne suggested idly.

'Oh gosh!' Mark exclaimed. 'What mugs we are! Of course the pedals can't move when the wheels are on the ground.'

'What?'

'Don't you see, this bike's fixed on its stand so the wheels are touching the floor. So the floor's acting as a brake all the time – of course the pedals won't work forwards, only backwards when they aren't connected to the wheels.'

'I see,' Marianne said. What she saw even more clearly was that this discovery was a relief to Mark's pride, since it established that no one, however strong and energetic, could have moved the pedals.

'Do you want to go upstairs again?' she asked. 'Shall I go first and open the door?'

'Yes, do, please,' Mark said. 'I think I'd like to go back to bed.'

He looked, suddenly, desperately tired.

'Would you like me to help you up?' Marianne asked.

'No, thanks. You go ahead.'

Marianne waited in the bedroom upstairs, a little anxious in case Mark should find he couldn't drag himself up the stairs, after so much unwonted effort. She sat on the window seat listening to the drag and shuffle of his approach. Then she glanced over her shoulder out of the window. She hadn't given a thought to anything outside the house since she had found herself there this time, she had been too much engrossed with Mark and the bicycle. Now as she looked, she saw that there was a difference from what she had seen last time. The watchers outside the fence no longer stood in ones or twos around the house – but in a solid rank, at most two or three feet apart. As Marianne looked an eyelid fell and was lifted again: another eye closed and opened. Each eye, as far as she could tell, was turned towards the lower window, the window of the room where the bicycle was standing. She moved, in an involuntary shudder. Immediately the heavy eyelids fell, one after another, opened again, and the eyes turned up and towards her.

Marianne stepped back into the room. She turned to the door and said, as he came in, 'Mark! THEY're watching us. They know about the bicycle and they're looking at us more than ever. We've got to get away or they'll try to stop us. We've got to be quick, Mark!' But she heard her voice in the haze of a dream, and it was only dimly that she saw Mark reach the side of the bed and say in the flat voice of complete exhaustion, 'I can't get up. I can't do any more.' Marianne saw him crumpled on the floor and moved to help him, but never reached the bed. She woke, instead, in her own.

15. The Voices

After all, the week which Marianne had thought was going to seem so terribly long, went as quickly as any other week of her stay in bed. Miss Chesterfield and she finished reading *A Tale Of Two Cities* and read *Treasure Island* for a complete change. Marianne mastered the principles of areas and volumes, in arithmetic, and was introduced to the decimal point. Thomas, her young brother, surprised everyone very much by coming second in a total scoring of points at his school Sports Day, and proudly brought home a very small silver cup, which he insisted should be lent to Marianne to have in her room for a week, to console her for the fact that she had not been able to witness his triumph. And, most important of all, Dr Burton was persuaded to say that possibly – 'but only possibly, you understand, depending on how you get on between now and then' – Marianne might get up at the beginning of the week after next for an hour. Marianne's father drew a beautiful calendar, ruled with green ink and lettered in black, with a red patterned ring round a Tuesday, which was to be the day. It hung by her bed, and every day Marianne scored off another square and felt another step nearer to being quite well again.

But while the day was taken up with real life happenings, Marianne did not neglect her dream life either. One of the charms of being an indifferent artist is that, while nothing you draw looks exactly as it was meant to, so it is possible to alter your original sketch to suit your needs without making it look any less lifelike. Marianne, by lengthening the bicycle stand and giving it rather more base than it had before, got the bicycle off the floor: and added, for convenience, a short pair of library steps with a hand rail, up which she thought Mark might be able to climb. After careful interrogation of Dr Burton, she put, both in the upstair and downstair rooms, the kind of rings hanging on ropes which one finds in gymnasiums, with which Mark could pull himself up from the floor to his bed or to the bicycle.

She felt rewarded for the trouble she had taken when, in her next dream, Mark said the moment she opened the door of his room, 'I've done it!'

'What?'

'Turned the wheels. With my feet. I say, Marianne, it was jolly clever of you to think of the rings and the ladder. They make a lot of difference.'

'Oh, good. And you really managed to do the pedals properly – forwards, I mean?'

'Yes. I took off my slipper and sort of hitched my toes round the pedal so I could pull it up as well as push it down with the good leg. And it works beautifully. It's a jolly good bike, too.'

'I'm frightfully glad,' Marianne said whole-heartedly. 'I'm sure it's going to make you better much more quickly. Do you think it's made any difference already?'

'I'm not sure. I did think today when I was practising downstairs, you know, that it seemed as if I could go on a bit longer without feeling quite so dead beat.'

Marianne discovered, in the following days, that in order to be sure to get back into the dream at night, she must draw with the pencil by day. So every day she added a small useful object to the already overcrowded rooms; and at night she and Mark now ate cold roast chicken and sausages with knives and forks and off plates. They played Monopoly and had a darts-board on the wall opposite the end of Mark's bed, and though he was not very good, Marianne was worse. And every time she saw him, Mark could report some improvement. Soon he could use his right leg almost as well as his left in turning the pedals. Later he told Marianne that he had climbed into the saddle with the help of the rings, but without the ladder. Marianne noticed that he was now hungry: he ate more of the chicken than she did; his legs and arms no longer looked wasted, useless things. He laughed more, teased more and could talk with less embarrassment of his weakness and with more conviction of getting well.

'By the way,' Miss Chesterfield said, as she was leaving, on the very day before the great Tuesday when Marianne was to be allowed up for the first time, 'Mark is home again. Did I tell you?'

'Home?' said Marianne. She saw Mark so frequently now that she had almost forgotten his separate existence in the waking world and had neglected to ask Miss Chesterfield about him for a long time. 'Do you mean he's come out of the iron lung?'

'Ages ago. Didn't I tell you that, either? Yes, he's been out of the lung for over two weeks now, and they said at the hospital that he'd made a remarkably good recovery and there was no need for him to have any more help with his breathing. They think he's really turned the corner now; he's better even than he was before he got that last cold and he's beginning to get some use back into his legs again.'

'Good,' was all that Marianne said, but it did not express half her inward satisfaction. Before she was due to go to sleep that night, she looked at her drawings and racked her brains to think of something else to add which would amuse Mark and ensure that she saw him again that night.

Both downstairs rooms were now almost as full as Mark's bedroom. But in the left-hand upstairs room, so far Marianne had drawn nothing, from some curious feeling that none of the useful and agreeable objects she wanted to introduce into the house would be quite fitting. It looked surprisingly empty beside the other three crowded rooms, and this evening Marianne began to draw in it only because there was no available space anywhere else. She drew, and it seemed an inspiration, a radio. It would be nice for Mark to listen to when she was not there, she thought. She could carry it into his room and put it on the floor beside his bed so that he could turn it on or off as he wanted.

She was surprised when she found herself in the dream to notice that it was dusk. Lately, it had never been darker than the half-light which seemed to be daylight there, but now it was clear that night was approaching. She was in an unfamiliar room too, empty, cold, with a curious fusty unpleasant smell, the smell of mouldy damp stone. Against one wall, looking out of place in its surroundings, stood a brand-new shiny radio cabinet.

Marianne left the room and walked across the landing to Mark's door. She gave a preliminary knock and had half opened the door, when Mark's voice said, 'Half a moment. Don't come in till I tell you.'

Marianne waited obediently, and a minute later when Mark's voice said, 'All right, come in,' she opened the door fully and stepped into the room.

Mark was standing by the bed.

'Wait!' he said, before she had time to speak. 'I want to show you something. Stay there by the door.'

He let go of the bedpost and took a step towards her: then another step, with the other leg, the weaker of the two. Then another with the left leg. Two more steps and he had reached Marianne, who put out her hands: but Mark shook his head without speaking, took one more step and touched the door, turned and faltered his way back to the bed again. Once there he pulled himself easily up by the rings and swung himself into bed. He grinned at Marianne.

'Surprised?'

'Frightfully. And I think it's wonderful.'

'Oh, no, not all that wonderful. I've been practising though, so I could do it before you knew I'd tried. I did it seven times this morning and I wasn't too tired, either.'

[132]

'Then you must be hungry,' Marianne said. 'I'll go and fetch the chicken.'

The chicken had, of course, to be fetched from the downstairs room where it had first appeared and where it always reappeared after being eaten. Marianne went down and collected the chicken, and the plates, knives and forks on a tray and brought them upstairs.

'There,' she said, putting the tray on the bed. 'You start. I'm not frightfully hungry, and I want to go and fetch something I've drawn for you.'

She went across the landing to the other room and took hold of the radio cabinet. To her surprise it did not move. A sharp tug made no difference, and, on examining it all round, she found it was fixed firmly to the wall.

'That's funny,' she thought. 'None of the other things have been fastened like this.'

'Mark!' she called out, 'I can't bring it because it's fastened in here, but I'll turn it on. Listen!'

[133]

She turned one of the two knobs and went quickly into Mark's room.

'Listen to what? I can't hear anything,' he said, his mouth full of chicken.

'It's a radio. I thought you'd like it. I expect it's warming up now; it must start soon.'

She held out her hand for the chicken, but dropped it again as a sound reached them from the farther room. It was a low booming noise, almost a growl, not continuous, but coming and going in snatches. Accompanying it, but going on all the time and much fainter, was a thin dry rustling sound, like that made when the wind blows through dry grass, or dead leaves shake on a tree.

'Ugh!' said Marianne shivering. 'I don't like that. I must have tuned it wrong. I'm sorry. I'll go and try again.'

She came back from the other room looking puzzled.

'There are only two knobs and one is what turns it on and the other makes it louder or softer. There isn't a tuning knob at all!'

'Perhaps there's only one station here,' Mark said reasonably. 'What happens when you turn it up?'

'Just the same noise, but louder. Only, Mark, it almost sounds as if the humming sort of noise might be words, only I can't understand them.'

'Turn it up really loud so I can hear.'

'All right. But I don't like it. I wish I'd never drawn it. And it's getting awfully dark.'

'Never mind,' Mark said, 'the light will be coming round soon.'

Marianne went back unwillingly into the other room. In spite of having no bars across its window it seemed even darker than the rest of the house. She turned up the volume control and immediately the house echoed with the low broken boom, and the rustle of dead grasses seemed to be in the room. She turned it down again.

'Not too much,' Mark's voice called from the other room.

[134]

'We want to be able to hear ourselves speak. But a bit louder than that.'

Marianne regulated the volume as well as she could. When she went back to Mark, the room was so dark she could hardly see to reach for her share of chicken on the plate on the bed.

'It's a very queer noise,' Mark said dubiously. 'It's not like any radio programme I've ever heard.'

'I don't like it,' Marianne said.

'Well, turn it off, then,' Mark began. But as he spoke the sound altered and at the same moment the radiance of the great golden beam from the lighthouse passed the window.

When it had passed Marianne stirred uneasily on the bed.

'I heard words!' she whispered.

'So did I.'

'And something else!'

'I wasn't sure. Was it music?'

'I wasn't sure, either!'

'Let's leave it on and listen again next time the light comes.'

They sat in silence. The low boom seemed more disjointed than ever; the rustling continued. Then, as the light swung round, each child heard distinctly the rumbling of harsh voices, which spoke all together. 'Not the light! Not the light! Not the light!' the voices said as it approached. For a moment as the light came fully outside the house, the voices and the rustling were silent; as it swept past they began but less distinct, uneven, as if shaken by the glare. And in that moment of silence, each child heard, infinitesimally far off, music, like the music of a trumpet a hundred miles away.

'It's THEM,' Marianne whispered. 'They don't like the light.'

'And the rustling is the grass outside.'

'We're hearing what THEY think. It's horrible.'

'Still, we know that you're right. THEY don't like the light,' Mark said.

'Yes. Mark, did you hear that other sound? Music? Very far away.'

'Yes, I did.'

'What do you think that is? It can't possibly be THEM talking.'

'I don't know. I agree, it can't be THEM, though. I think it might be something to do with the light. It comes at the same time.'

'I do hope it is.'

'Let's hope THEY don't like music any more than light,' Mark said.

'There seems to be an awful lot of them,' Marianne said, shivering. 'There are lots of voices.'

'There couldn't be any more, could there?' Mark said dubiously. 'Aren't there just the number you drew at first?'

'I'm not sure. Last time I looked out – it was a long time ago – there seemed to be more. But it might just have been that it was more this side of the house, and that some had come round from the other side.'

'Could they move, do you think?'

'I don't know. I'll look out next time the light comes.'

She felt her way round the bed and across to the window, and as she reached it the sounds from the radio told her that the light must be coming. The low hum broke more frequently, the whisper of the grasses became more agitated and sibilant, and as Marianne took a quick look round the window-frame, the garden and plain were flooded with light and the low voices said urgently together, 'Not the light! Not the light! Not the light!'

When it was dark again Marianne went back to the bed.

'Well,' said Mark's voice in the darkness.

'Mark, there are more of them! Much more. And they're closer.'

'How can they be closer? They were only just outside the fence before.'

'Yes, but now they're inside. Some of them are!'

'Right up to the house?'

'Not quite. But they're coming. Mark, do you think they know we're planning to get away and mean to stop us?'

'I suppose so!' Mark's voice was gloomy. 'And I should think they'll manage it. I can't see how we can get out if there are so many of THEM all just outside.'

'We'd have to get out while they shut their eyes, like I said before. But I'm not going without you. You'll have to come, Mark. If they can get right up to the house they might get in and then –'

She stopped.

'All right,' Mark said.

'You'll come? You'll try?'

'Not tonight. I must practise a bit more or I wouldn't have a chance. I'm quite good on the bike, but I must be able to walk a bit more.'

'Very well,' Marianne said, a little disappointed. 'When do you think you'll be ready?'

'I don't know exactly. Time's funny here. I think it goes quicker than I'm used to, because if I practise something one day I seem to be able to do it, very often, the next.'

'Perhaps in a few days,' Marianne urged. 'We've got to be quick, because of THEM.'

'I know. I'll practise hard.'

After a moment, he said, 'Marianne!'

'What?'

'There's one thing you haven't thought of, isn't there?'

'What?'

'Where are we going to?'

It was certainly something Marianne had never considered: yet, without knowing she was going to, she answered at once, 'To the lighthouse first and then to the sea.'

She couldn't tell whether it was her certainty or because Mark saw himself that it was the only possible answer, that he agreed at once, 'Yes, of course.'

'I wonder if we'll need anything else when we go,'

Marianne said. 'I could draw some extra things if you can think of them.'

'You ought to have a bike, too. Can you ride?'

'Yes. But I don't think there's room to put another one in.'

'Not anywhere in the house?'

'Not in any of the rooms, except the one where the radio is and I don't want to put it there, it would turn out wrong somehow, like that did.'

'What about in the hall?'

'Yes, that's a good idea. Anything else?'

Mark considered. 'Bicycle baskets,' he said. 'We ought to be able to carry food with us.'

'We could take the chicken.'

'And some sausages.'

'And the eggs.'

They both laughed. For perhaps the fourth time since Marianne had left the window the murmur of the radio rose to a babble, the light swept round and the proud distant music sounded in the instant of silence, before the rustle and the voices began again.

'I hate that noise,' Mark said uneasily. 'Couldn't you turn it off?'

'I suppose I could,' Marianne said. She was very unwilling to go into that dark room again.

'I wish you would,' Mark said.

'It's awfully dark.'

'But you know just where it is, don't you? Couldn't you feel your way there and back?'

'I'll try,' said Marianne, with a sinking heart.

She went out of Mark's room on to the dark landing and felt her way along the wall to the room opposite. She went through the open door and saw a dim light coming from the black hulk of the radio. In here, close to it, in the dark, the booming voices were more distinct. Marianne thought she could distinguish words, though so broken and confused still she could not be sure. 'Watching' . . . 'I am watching' . . .

'Watch' . . . 'We watch them,' she thought she heard. She put out her hand to turn the knob, but at that moment, suddenly, the boom increased, became rhythmical with terror. 'Not the light! Not the light! Not the light!' cried the voices, boring into Marianne's ears and hammering the sides of her head. She stepped back, cried out, 'No!' and then in the moment of silence and music, turned the knob. In the following quiet and darkness, she woke.

16. The Escape

Dr Burton came early on Tuesday morning, and pronounced Marianne fit to get up; so that afternoon, for the first time for more than two months, she put on her clothes and sat in a chair for an hour. At first, although her legs felt feeble, it was a delightful and exciting adventure: but after quite a short time it palled. Sitting in a chair was in some mysterious way much more exhausting than sitting up in bed, and it was not funny, after the first time, to try to stand up and find oneself on the floor because one's legs simply wouldn't carry one. Before the hour was up, Marianne was aching to be back in bed, and when she finally got there it was with tears of weariness and despair.

'Never mind,' said Dr Burton, who had called in at the end of his evening round to see how she had got on. 'You're bound to be tired after the first time up. I expect you wish you were dead, don't you? Everyone does when they have their first outing after two months in bed. Now tomorrow you can do exactly the same as you did tonight, then on Thursday make it an hour and a half.'

Marianne thought, but didn't say then, that she never wanted to get up again; she would rather stay quietly in bed for ever than feel so battered by fatigue. She slept without dreaming that night, and the next day, to her great surprise, found that she had quite recovered and was even looking forward to her hour out of bed. But again she was exhausted by the evening, too tired to draw, too tired to think about Mark, too tired even to remember the other world where so much was happening.

'Tomorrow you shall stay up for longer,' her mother said, as she tucked her up. 'You really are getting on, darling. I'm so glad.'

'I'm not,' Marianne said gloomily, as she straightened her aching back in the bed. 'And I don't want to stay up for an extra half-hour. I feel like jelly after just one hour and I should think I'll die if I have to stay up longer.'

'I don't think it'll be quite as drastic as that,' her mother said, laughing and kissing her. 'We'll see tomorrow, anyhow. Sleep well, Marianne, darling. Have nice dreams.'

But that night again Marianne had no dreams.

Thursday started badly. It was a grey depressing-looking morning and directly after breakfast Miss Chesterfield rang up to say that she was very sorry but she had a streaming summer cold and wouldn't be able to come. So there was a whole morning to get through, with nothing particular to do, and the doubtful pleasure of getting up to look forward to in the afternoon.

At about eleven o'clock it began to rain steadily; a fine drizzling downpour that looked as if it might go on for ever. Marianne felt that this was more than she could bear. She had been half-heartedly reading one of the Arthur Ransome books; but she knew it too well already to be really engrossed, and when the steady patter of the rain on the leaves outside had been going on for some time, she pushed it away from her impatiently. All the characters in the book were so active and well, they annoyed her; it seemed to emphasize her own feebleness. She lay for some time looking out of the window at the sheets of rain with very disagreeable reactions.

'I don't want to get up this afternoon,' she said to herself.

'I hate feeling tired all the time, and it isn't like being properly well. It's neither one thing nor the other, not being well and not being ill, and I hate it. I suppose that's how Mark felt the first time he got out of bed, but I didn't know then what it was like. I'm not surprised he was so cross. I feel cross. Very.'

[141]

It cheered her a little, however, to remember that Mark had been feebler than she was when he had first got up, and he had got stronger very quickly. 'But that's in a dream,' she thought, 'and time is different there. I'm sure it takes me longer to get well here than it does Mark there. I wonder how he's getting on?'

She remembered suddenly how very important it was that Mark should get on quickly in the house surrounded by Watchers. She pulled out her drawing book, found the pencil, and in the hall of the house she drew a bicycle which she hoped would turn out the right size for her. She added baskets to both machines, Mark's and her own, and then looked at her drawing of the road winding up to the hills. It looked extraordinarily naked; she drew in some bushes and a few trees in the foreground, but it seemed to her that the distant part of the road should remain as bare as the hills it climbed. She put a tiny door at the bottom of the lighthouse: it was essential they should be able to get inside. She was pleased with herself for thinking of this and was encouraged to draw a plan of what she thought the inside of a lighthouse might look like. Long, long ago she had been shown over one in Cornwall, but all she could remember now was an enormous number of steps leading up to the light at the top. She divided the tower into two large circular rooms and made the stair go up, as well as she could, through both, and up to the dome where the light came from. She drew electric lights in both the rooms and was engaged in putting in a tiny carpet with a very elaborate pattern, when her mother surprised her by coming in and announcing that she had finished all her shopping and cooking and could read aloud or play cards, or any game that Marianne chose, till lunch.

'I suppose I am getting better,' Marianne said doubtfully, as she got back into bed that evening, after her hour and a half of being up.

'Much better,' her mother said firmly. 'I can see that you aren't as tired tonight as you were yesterday, and you've been up for longer, you know.'

'It's awfully slow,' Marianne said, sighing.

'I'm afraid getting quite well after such a long illness is bound to be slow,' her mother said. 'But Dr Burton thinks you are getting on quite quickly enough. He especially doesn't want you to hurry.'

'Shouldn't I do some exercises to get my legs strong again?' Marianne asked, thinking of Mark. 'I could sort of bicycle in the air to work my muscles, or touch my toes, or do somersaults on the bed.'

'Not yet,' her mother said. 'Perhaps later. But for the present you must just stay where you are and only get up a little more every day.'

'Supposing,' Marianne thought, as she settled herself for sleep that night, 'I can't bicycle now, in the dream? I shouldn't be able to go with Mark when he's ready. And I haven't bicycled since I was ill, so I might not be able to. But I can walk there and I can't here, so perhaps I can ride a bicycle there, though I'm not allowed to here. Anyway, I'm sure Mark wouldn't go and leave me in the house all by myself.'

She found herself, as she had known she would, in the hall, in front of her bicycle, which was propped up against a wall. As far as she could tell it was complete, including the basket. She gave an experimental spin to the back wheel, and was just going upstairs when a noise attracted her attention. It was not the radio: but from the front room to the right of the stairs, came a whirring sound which Marianne could not identify.

'It's THEM!' was her immediate thought. 'They've got in and they're doing something in there. I wonder if that's the sort of noise a time-bomb makes. I must go and warn Mark.'

But before she had reached more than half-way up the stairs the noise stopped. The door of the room opened and Mark came out. He walked slowly but steadily to the door of the room opposite, opened it, and then, without seeing Marianne, went back into the room he had just come from. There was a sound of scraping, of something heavy being set down with a thud and then suddenly a flurry of broken china, and Mark rode out of one door, on his bicycle, and across the hall and into the room opposite. A moment later he was back in the hall again and had disappeared into the room he had come from. There was a sound of more china breaking; and Mark's voice said, 'Bother these eggs!'

Marianne clapped her hands as if she were applauding at a play.

Mark's head appeared out of the door; his face wore a slightly alarmed expression, which changed to relief when he saw Marianne.

'Hullo! I didn't know you'd got here! Did you see the round tour?'

'Yes, it's marvellous! You must have been practising awfully hard.'

'I have. Like to see me do it again?'

'Yes, please.'

[144]

She followed him into the room and saw the bicycle on its stand surrounded by broken china and squashed hard-boiled eggs.

'It is rather a mess,' Mark said apologetically. 'But there isn't much room, and if I start trying to get out of their way I fall off. When I broke them the first time I was in an awful state about it, but the next day they were all there just as good as ever, so now I don't bother about them.'

He lifted the bicycle to the ground.

'Stand clear! Run after me and you can see.'

He repeated the route he had taken before. This time he did not get off when he reached his starting-point, but went on riding until he had been in and out of each room half a dozen times. When he finally dismounted Marianne was surprised to see that he did not seem tired or breathless.

'All right,' Mark said, stretching his arms and legs. 'Let's go upstairs. The chicken's up there already.'

He walked upstairs vigorously too, his right leg only a very little less active than his left. When they were back in his room, sitting on the side of his bed and eating the chicken, Marianne said, 'You've got on awfully quickly, Mark.'

'Do you think so?' he said. 'I've practised like anything since you were here last. I suppose I haven't done so badly.'

'Then can we go?'

'Go?'

'Get out of here. Go to the lighthouse. I do think we ought to, Mark. I'm sure it isn't safe to stay.'

'You're in such a hurry,' Mark complained. 'I've only just started really riding the bike. I ought to do a bit more practice first.'

'I think we ought to go now,' Marianne insisted.

'Why the hurry?'

'It's partly a feeling, partly that I know it isn't safe to stay here. Every time I come back here it feels more dangerous: and we do know that – that THEY are getting closer. Why won't you go?'

'Because I'm not ready yet,' Mark said irritably. 'You want to rush things so. Anyhow you don't know that THEY are any closer this time. You haven't looked yet.'

'Have you?'

'No. I tell you, I'm not interested in them. I just want to get absolutely back to normal here, then I'll go like a shot.'

'I'm going to look now,' Marianne said. She could see that Mark was too much excited by his newly found powers on the bicycle to be able to think of anything else.

She went over to the window and looked carefully out. The usual half-light prevailed outside; beyond the garden fence were now not just a few, but ranks of Watchers: the fence had been completely broken down in several places and now only a few yards from the house were five or six enormous stones. But what frightened Marianne, more even than their proximity, was the air of expectancy, of waiting for some event just about to happen, which she could sense from one quick glance. The eyes, she thought, moved a fraction more quickly, the eyeballs swung to and fro as if the Watchers were aware that the activity inside the house had increased, and they were more alert themselves to guard against it.

'Mark!' Marianne said, coming back to the bed and instinctively dropping her voice. 'They are much nearer. They're almost up to the house and they look more awake. More as if they were waiting to catch us.'

'Let me look,' Mark said. Less cautious than Marianne, he walked up to the middle of the window but almost immediately drew sharply to the side, and then came slowly back to the bed.

'Well?' Marianne asked.

'I must say I'd forgotten how beastly THEY are,' Mark admitted.

'And there are a lot of them very close, aren't there?'

'Yes, they are a bit too close.'

'Then don't you think we ought to go?'

'I – don't – know,' Mark said slowly. 'I don't want to try

to get out and find I can't make it, but I agree with you, I don't want to stay here longer than we can help.'

'What shall we do then?'

'Let's wait till it's dark and then decide. If THEY come any nearer before then we'll know how fast they're moving and we can think what's best to do.'

'When will it be dark?' Marianne asked.

'I don't know,' Mark said. 'I never know here. Sometimes when I'm here it's light all the time, and other times it's mostly dark and sometimes it changes. We'll have to wait and see.'

Marianne had never been in the house for so long before: nor had any time of waiting seemed so endless as the long day that dragged on as she and Mark waited for the night to come. Sitting on the bed, on the floor, on the stairs for a change, they played all the card games they knew, they played draughts, they played chess, they played Monopoly twice through, they even played noughts and crosses. Every now and then one of them would take a quick survey through a window, careful to keep out of sight themselves. The Watchers seemed to be no nearer; but even Mark admitted to feeling their unrest and expectancy. The atmosphere in the house grew tense: both Mark and Marianne became more bored and irritable as time passed and the half-light outside persisted in its pale hard sameness. It seemed as if the dark would never come.

'You can't move your king and your castle together after the king has been checked,' Mark said sharply, as they were playing their third game of very inexpert chess.

'Yes, I can! It doesn't make any difference whether he's been checked or not!'

'No, it's one of the rules that you can't castle if your king has been in check.'

'But I always play like this.'

'Then you always play wrong,' said Mark disagreeably.

'I don't! Anyhow, my father taught me how to play and he knows better than you.'

'Then your father simply doesn't know the rules any more than you do.'

'He does! And anyhow I'm going to castle,' Marianne said, moving the pieces.

'You can't! Put them back and play properly!'

'I won't.'

'All right then, I will,' Mark said. He leant across and reached for Marianne's king. At the same moment Marianne moved the board sideways to get it out of his reach. Mark's arm caught the taller pieces and swept them to the floor.

'Now look what you've done!' Marianne said triumphantly.

'You're obviously,' Mark said, in a voice that trembled with rage and sarcasm, 'much too young to play an adult game like chess. I should think tiddlywinks would be much more suitable for your age.'

He slid off the bed, with the chessmen's box in his hand and felt about for the pieces that had dropped. Suddenly, in a completely different tone, he said, 'Marianne!'

'What?' said Marianne, still furious.

'I can't see properly to pick the chessmen up.'

Marianne looked quickly round the room and out of the window and saw that at last the pale light had begun to fade. Outside it was like a winter twilight: in the room it was already so dark that, as Mark had said, it was difficult to distinguish one object from another.

'It's getting dark!' she breathed.

Mark retrieved the last chessmen and stood up.

'Thank goodness for that. We seem to have been waiting hours. Now what?'

He slid the chessmen back into their box.

'I think we ought to turn the radio on.'

'Oh, no!' Marianne cried out. 'Don't let's have it! It's horrible! It frightens me!'

'Yes, I know. But it could be useful. Don't you remember what you said the first time we heard it? It tells us what THEY are thinking.'

[148]

He left the room and Marianne heard him go into the room opposite. He was back immediately.

'I do think you're brave!' Marianne said. 'I hate going into that room.'

For answer Mark only held up his finger to encourage her to listen. Quietly at first, then louder and louder, came the intermittent booming, broken into almost distinguishable words and behind it the continuous sibilant rustle of dry grass, dead leaves or snakes crossing dusty earth.

Marianne shivered. Unexpectedly Mark put an arm roughly round her shoulders for a moment.

'It's all right,' he said. 'THEY're outside still, you know. And the light will be here in a minute.'

He had hardly said the words when the booming voices rose in pitch and excitement, became more discordant and more distinct in their protest. 'Not the light! Not the light! Not the light!' And then, in the silence of the boom and the rustle, as the golden glow went past, Marianne and Mark heard not only the joyful music from the distance, but also, in the music, a voice, a voice to be implicitly trusted, believed in and followed. It said, 'Go. Now. Go. Now. Go. Now. Go.'

As the light fled and the disturbed protesting hum returned, Mark said, 'All right. I think you were right. Let's go.'

'Now?'

'As soon as we can. Come on.'

'But, Mark! You've only got pyjamas! And we haven't packed the bicycle baskets! And we've eaten the chicken!'

'We'll take sausages and eggs,' Mark said practically. 'I expect I'll be all right in pyjamas. Anyway, I haven't got anything else – unless you've drawn me something?'

'I'm sorry, I never thought about it. And, Mark, we haven't –'

'Look!' said Mark, sternly. 'You've been saying all the time we ought to go and there isn't much time and it's dangerous to stay here. Now I'm agreeing with you. I think it's dangerous. Too dangerous to stay any longer. We've got to get out now, while we can, I'm sure of that. But now you're trying to wait about and put off going. Come on, Marianne! It may be beastly getting out, but I'm sure it would be even more beastly if we stayed.'

'Yes,' said Marianne. 'Let's go.'

'Can you see the sausages or the eggs?'

'No. But I can feel them. I've got all the sausages and about four eggs. I can't carry any more.'

'Good. Let's go down then.'

'Mark, wouldn't it be a good idea –'

She broke off as the sounds from the radio increased in volume again. 'Not the light! Not the light!' said some of the voices: but others, joining in the discordant chorus said, 'What? Look out! What? Look out!' Then the music followed, and the great voice said, more urgently this time than before, 'Go. Now. Go. Now. Go. Now. Now. Now. Now.'

Marianne and Mark moved simultaneously to the door. On the way Marianne remembered what she had just been going to say.

'Mark!' she whispered. 'Wouldn't it be a good idea to take a blanket with us? In case you're cold?'

'Jolly good. Come on, I've got it.'

They went downstairs, stepping quietly without meaning to, as if the booming, whispering radio set upstairs could hear them.

'Have you found your bike?' Mark hissed.

'No, not yet. Bother. Yes, I have. I scraped against it.'

'Put the food in your basket and I'll take the blanket if I can.'

Marianne heard the crunch of eggshells and broken china as Mark groped his way through the room to his bicycle. A minute later she heard the soft click of well-oiled wheels as he wheeled it out to her in the hall.

'Ready?' he whispered.

'Yes. But, Mark, how are we going to do it?'

'Open the door when the light's there and make a dash for it while THEY have their beastly eyes shut.'

'Will we have time, do you think? With bicycles?'

'We'll have to go one at a time. Listen to the radio and be ready to go directly THEY stop talking. That'd give one of us time to get out with a bicycle.'

'What about the other one?'

'The first one to go must lie down in the grass to hide. Outside the gate if they can get there. We'll be able to see because of the light.'

'Who's to go first?'

'Would you rather? I will if you like.'

'I don't know,' Marianne said. 'I'd hate to be left – Mark! The light!'

Upstairs the radio, booming and rustling, was sending out the clearest words they had yet heard. 'Not the light! Not the light!' said one chorus. 'Look! Watch! Look! Watch!' said another. And a new mutter, very low and quiet, but full of menace. 'Get them! Get them! Get them!'

If Marianne had had time to listen she would never have had the courage, hearing those voices, to go. But as they rose in pitch and stopped, Mark had pulled open the door, pushed her out with her bicycle and shut the door behind her. There were four or five yards of shadow immediately outside the house: beyond lay the turning light. Marianne ran to the gate, trying not to see the stony watchers all around, each quivering stony eyelid held fast shut against the light: she wrenched it open, saw the shaft of light move and a wall of darkness approach, threw the bicycle away from her and flung herself down in the long grass.

In the total darkness which followed she could hear the hiss of the hostile grass which hid her. Low angry mutterings and stealthy movements on all sides and, louder than any of these, the quick beat of her own heart like a drum roll in her ears.

She wondered if she could bear to lie there, without

moving, unable to see, in the country of the enemy: but the fear that made her want to run away kept her still. The seconds passed: Marianne, hardly knowing it, counted sixty heart-beats. Then the grass rustled louder, more sibilantly,

the movements stopped and the muttering rumbled louder: raising her head a little, Marianne saw a great fan-shaped area of yellow light sweep round from a tower up high, far away. An instant later she was lying in a field of golden grass, and she saw Mark slip neatly out of the house door, wheel his bicycle to the gate, between the stone figures, and throw himself, as she had done, into hiding before the shaft of light had gone.

In the new darkness she wriggled across to the point where she had seen Mark last.

'Mark!' she whispered very low.

'Marianne! Be careful. There are lots of THEM round us!'

'When shall we go?'

'Move a little. Every time the light comes. When THEY can't see us. Get ready next time. Towards the light. Meet on the road!'

'Bicycle?'

'Not yet. Not safe. Just wheel.'

They lay silent. Marianne wondered if their conversation had been covered by the hiss of the grass; or had it been transmitted to the Watchers by the whispering stalks? She could hear the voice of the radio booming above the stealthy sounds round her, and as the light approached again, the voices had new words. 'Look! Watch! Look! Watch!' they said, as before: and 'Where? Gone! Where? Gone! Get them! Get them! Get them!' Then all together, 'Not the light! Not the light! Not the light!'

It was the signal. Marianne crawled to her bicycle, picked it up and was running with it, as well as she could, as soon and as long as the beam was on her. She ran towards the source of light, over stony, uneven ground, pushing her way against the grass, which beat on her skirt and whipped her legs with little stinging lashes. She had also to look, as she ran, for the Watchers, grouped here and there, now in twos, now in sevens or eights. She was still not far from the house when the light passed and she lay again on the ground. From the panting breathing she could hear not far off, she imagined that Mark was somewhere near: but she dared not speak. She had not had time to see clearly how she was surrounded as she had thrown herself down. She put out a hand and touched stones and earth; then the long harsh stalks of the grass: then her fingers met something cold, damp, unyielding, and yet in some indescribable way alive. She felt the withdrawal, the shrinking of the stone and had snatched back her hand before the Thing cried out. For, as if her touching it had set off some alarm, suddenly the air all around her was filled with a vibration, a savage horrifying roar of fear and hate, which Marianne could feel beating against her ear-drums and temples, but yet could not hear as she could hear the savage hiss of the grass rising to a shrill whistle, and the boom from the radio in the house behind her.

She felt Mark's hand on her arm.

'That's torn it,' he said. 'THEY know. We've got to go.'

'Next time the light comes?'

'No, now. If we stay here they'll kill us. Get on your bike and just go. I'll catch you up in the light.'

Marianne felt with a shudder for her bicycle and thankfully found its good solid metal bars and nothing more. She turned her back on the boom and the hiss, mounted and rode in the dark, not knowing where or how she went, not caring, if only she could get away from the intolerable pressure on her ears and head – it was like being surrounded by the deepest pipes of the organ, which can be felt but hardly heard. A thousand great bells, harsh and savage, beat in her brain and she fled, not noticing the bumping of the bicycle over stony uneven ground, losing her sense of direction, pursued by panic.

For a moment or two the pressure on her head lifted as the light came and went. As it passed she felt a hand over hers on the handlebars, turning them slightly. She had opened her mouth to shriek, when she heard Mark's voice in her ear.

'A bit more to the left. We've got to go straight towards the light.'

'Oh, Mark! Don't go away! I can't bear it! It's terrible!'

'It's all right. We've just got to get on as fast as we can. We'll keep together, then you won't go wrong again.'

'How do you know which way to go?' asked Marianne, calming down a little.

'You can see the lighthouse properly now, even when the light isn't coming this way. Look!'

Up on an invisible skyline, a wheel seemed to be searching the sky: its spokes were golden light, between the spokes was black velvet. Marianne saw and recognized their destination.

It was impossible to bicycle fast: the ground was not only stony, but ridged like a ploughed field. Sometimes the ridges ran parallel to their path, sometimes across: and always the way lay slightly uphill. When the light came round they could go a little faster, but their progress in the dark was very slow, and there was a great deal of dark. Marianne heard Mark panting beside her and she could feel that his hold on her handlebars instead of helping her on, as it had at first, had become a brake on her progress. She was, in fact, pulling him with her. But the pressure on her ears had lessened, the voices were faint and indistinct, and though the grass still hissed, and stung their legs, it was not enough to hold them back; and the light, when it came, showed fewer of the watchers among the stalks and the house farther and farther behind them.

'Mark!' said Marianne, after what seemed like a long time of this painful journey. 'I'm tired. We can't go on much longer like this.'

She had been going to say 'you're tired', but changed it out of respect for Mark's feelings.

'No!' Mark said. He spoke in gasps, his breath coming very short. 'We can't. But . . . we must keep on. For the moment.'

'How far? When can we stop?'

'Didn't you. Say. There was. A road somewhere? Up to. The lighthouse?'

'Yes!' Marianne exclaimed. 'And trees. Or bushes, any-way. If we could get there, we could hide in the bushes for a bit. Good. Come on.'

She pedalled with renewed vigour, but was more and more conscious of Mark's weight holding her back. He was pedalling, but feebly, his breathing was uneven, and when she saw his face in the light, Marianne was shocked. It was drawn into an expression of intense fatigue: his eyes seemed to have sunk into his head. Only his mouth was set in a thin line, but it was a line of determination and despair.

He saw her look and tried to smile.

'Can you see the road?'

'I'll look next time.'

They rode in silence: and it was now almost a complete silence. Far away Marianne could hear the boom, very faintly against her ear-drums she could feel the beat of that savage roar: but the preponderant sound was the harsh whistle of the grass, the bump of their machines over ruts and stones, and their own laboured breathing. Once, twice, the great light swung past and showed them only the grassy plain ahead. The third time Marianne saw a glimmer of white bordered with something dark. Without speaking she turned slightly towards it, Mark turning with her. And suddenly, in the dark again, the wheels of the bicycles ran easily, even a little downhill, on a smooth, gritty, road surface. Marianne had just seen dark trees on each side of her, and felt the relief of being free from those singing grasses, when Mark's bicycle suddenly shook and his front wheel ran into her. She had time to spring off her own machine and half catch him as he fell sideways towards her. She dragged him clear of their bicycles, to the side of the road and under the trees, rescued the tangle of bicycles from the road, flung herself down, panting, bruised, exhausted, beside Mark; and stopped dreaming.

17. The End of the Road

When she dreamed again the next night, after a day which seemed, in comparison, so unreal that she had gone through it as if that were the dream and this the only reality, she found herself again in the dark, lying on short harsh turf; and it seemed so perfectly natural to be there that she said, without hesitation, 'Mark.'

'Yes, I'm here. Good, I'm glad you are, too.'

'How long have you been here?'

'I don't know. Not very long. The light has been round about twelve or fifteen times since I came.'

'And you had a day in between, too?'

'I don't know,' Mark said slowly. 'I told you, when I'm here I don't seem to know properly about anything else. I can't remember what happens when I'm not here.'

'Are you all right now?'

'I think so. What happened before we got here? I can't remember the end of it. How did we get into this sort of grass? It's not like the other. And there are trees all round, and the road's just there.'

The light flooded them as he spoke. Marianne saw that Mark was sitting near her, wrapped in the blanket he had taken off his bed.

She was relieved to notice that his face had begun to look more normal and had lost the sunken, exhausted look it had worn before.

'You were awfully tired,' she said. 'I think you must have fainted. You fell off your bicycle, so I pulled you in here. That's all.'

'Sorry to be so feeble,' Mark said roughly.

'Don't be silly. You were probably right about wanting more time to practise before we started, but we had to get out quickly. I thought it was marvellous you could do as much as you did.'

'Thanks. I don't, though, I think it was futile.'

'Let's have something to eat,' Marianne suggested. She felt for her bicycle and found it. 'Isn't it funny?' she said, munching. 'How the first thing I always do when I come here – to the house or here, I mean – is to eat? I always seem to arrive hungry.'

'Don't blame you,' Mark said, his mouth full. 'I'm ravenous.'

'We've come quite a long way,' Marianne remarked.

'Not so very, really. You can see the house when the light comes round, and it's not very far off. By the way, I meant to warn you, don't talk loudly. There are some of THEM about.'

'Here?'

'Not right on top of us, but not far off. I saw one through the trees behind us and I'm almost sure there's another on the road.'

'I thought we shouldn't see any more. I thought we'd be safe now.'

'I shouldn't think so, at all. And I think we ought to get on, Marianne. I'm not at all sure I didn't see THEM coming up from the house – not fast, but just a lot of them.'

Marianne put down the sausage she was eating, suddenly no longer hungry, and looked towards the house, as if her eyes could pierce the dark. When the light had spread its wing over the country, and gone again, she got up.

'Let's go.'

Mark swallowed half a hard-boiled egg and pulled his bicycle towards him.

'All right. I'm ready.'

'Where is the – the one of THEM you saw on the road?'

'I'm not sure. Wait till it's light again, and we'll see before we start riding. Keep behind the bushes.'

They waited. Marianne was aware, for the first time since she had returned, of the distant reverberating beat in her ears: and the hiss of the long grass, so lately all around, was still audible. The boom had been left behind with the radio set apparently, but she knew, because in the last shaft of light she had seen, that the Watchers were still watching: between the tall grasses she had seen their grey shapes and hateful closed eyes. The house behind them was deserted by more than herself and Mark: the Watchers had come too.

The light, when it came, showed one Watcher only on the road before them; at Mark's sign, Marianne had mounted her bicycle and had followed him past the squat figure while it was still blinded by the light. They rode on. In the nearly complete darkness they could see the whiteness of the road just enough to follow it, though every shape that loomed at them from the side might be a harmless bush or might be one of THEM. Each time the light came round they could see what lay ahead: more than once they put on a spurt to get past a stone eye while it was still closed. The road lay uphill almost continuously. Marianne felt their pace becoming increasingly slower as the steepness of the incline increased. The beat in her ears was louder; she was not sure that it might not be her own heart-beat, but it was too much like the roar she had heard before to be reassuring.

The hill they were climbing became suddenly much steeper. Marianne swerved and stopped.

'Mark, I can't ride up here any more. I'll have to stop and walk!'

'All right.' Mark got off his bicycle, breathing hard. 'We'll walk this bit and ride again later.'

'I can't see as much,' Marianne said. 'I walked into a bush just then. I can't even see the side of the road properly and I could before. Why, do you think?'

'I don't know.'

The light swept over their heads, illuminating the road behind them, but not in front. Their way ahead seemed to

[159]

lie in denser shadow and even as the beam shone out at its fullest it no longer fell on them.

'The light!' Marianne said in terror. 'It's left us! We aren't in it any longer!'

'It's all right,' Mark said. 'There's a hill or something between us and it, that's all. It's going to be darker for a bit while we get up to the top. But keep going, we mustn't stop.'

They walked on. But the bicycles were surprisingly heavy to wheel up what was becoming a very steep hill, Mark's steps became uneven: Marianne could hear that he was limping, and though he tried, as his quick breathing showed, to keep pace with her, he was falling behind unless she slowed. As she listened to his footsteps halting on the road, Marianne heard another sound, mingled with the beat in her head, but different from it. It was the sound of steps behind, plodding, slow, like the pounding of a giant pestle in a huge mortar, but getting louder and nearer as the roar in her ears increased in volume and savagery, too.

'Mark,' she cried aloud.

'You go!' he said. 'I can't. Leave the bike. Run!'

'No!' cried Marianne. She dropped her bicycle in the road and ran round to the other side of Mark and put her arm round under his armpits. She pushed his bicycle to lie on top of her own.

'We'll walk,' she said. 'We can't take the bicycles. Come on.'

Mark let her support him, but as the stony tread came nearer still behind them, he said again, 'You go.'

'No! Run!'

'Can't.'

'You must.'

They broke into a lopsided, halting run. Farther back on the road the roar swelled suddenly. There was the sound of metal clashing on metal, and a snarl of disappointed rage.

'They're – breaking – our – bikes!' Mark gasped.

'Don't talk. Run!' Marianne urged, for already, after that brief halt she heard the renewed thud of their pursuers. She gasped herself as she ran: her arm ached with Mark's weight, and the stitch in her side was intolerably sharp. The blood pounded in her ears so that she could hardly distinguish what was in and what was outside her head, and she felt that her lungs must burst with each breath she took. Mark was panting as he stumbled beside her: his breathing came in deep groans. Several times his left foot caught on the road and he would have fallen if Marianne had not held him up. He muttered something between the groans, which Marianne could not hear.

'What?'

He could not summon enough breath to answer, but she felt him struggle. At first she thought it was for breath, but then she realized he was trying to free himself from her arm. He was pulling away from her in an effort to make her go on by herself and leave him to the mercy of their pursuers.

'No!' cried Marianne, with an energy she had not known she possessed. 'I won't go alone!'

She pulled him up from his half-sinking position as she

spoke. They took four, five, six, stumbling steps upwards, so steep it was almost climbing. And then suddenly, as a roar of defeated hate rose like a wave behind them, they had topped the hill. Before them, perhaps a quarter of a mile off, along level ground, stood the great tower, its domed top streaming forth light. As they stood there, they were bathed fully, completely in its golden rays; and to Marianne it seemed as if her last protesting cry, wrung from the bottom of her lungs and heart, had been caught up into the music of the light and been turned into a glorious, triumphant song.

They were on the crest of the hill. Below and behind them was darkness, with long snakes of grass, the empty house, the pale winding road and the halted Watchers, who dared not come up into the light. To their right, along the ridge, the road led to the base of the tower. Below and beyond the hills it was dark again, but it was a moving, living darkness, and Marianne could hear, far below, the splash and tinkle of little waves, the surge and withdrawal of surf on a stony shore.

A fresh salty wind blew into the children's faces from the sea. Mark took long deep breaths; his head lifted from his chest, and strength seemed to flow back into his limbs. Slowly, supporting each other, they walked towards the tower. When they reached it they turned the handle on the heavy door. The door swung open silently on its hinges and they stepped inside.

18. In the Tower

Marianne had never been so conscious of living two lives at once as in the days and nights that followed their escape.

By day, in her waking life, she was convalescent, up from bed for two, three hours, half a day; learning to get used to walking from one room to another, up and down the stairs – very difficult this – without stumbling, coming down to ordinary meals at ordinary times, and facing the difficult problem of behaving ordinarily and leading about half an ordinary life, while still being liable to attacks of sudden extraordinary tiredness and irritability. Lessons went on with Miss Chesterfield, now recovered from her cold: but they were lessons with the end in sight and directed towards that end, for when the next term began, Marianne was to go back to school and would be quite well again.

Getting well is sometimes more tiresome than being ill and completely in bed. The routine one has got used to as an invalid disappears, and instead there seems to be endless sitting uncomfortably in chairs, waiting for it to be time to go to bed again, after longing from the bed to be up in the chair: endless exhaustion following unwonted exercise: and a longing to be completely one thing or the other, well or ill, instead of someone hovering between the two, conscious all the time of the possible effect of every action, yet impelled to try to be active.

While the days passed in this useful but unsatisfactory way, Marianne's nights were spent in the tower on the hills. She had very quickly furnished it, with the help of The Pencil, with everything that she and Mark needed: and most nights when she went to sleep, she was sure of waking up in one of the two big circular rooms where Mark was always waiting for her. Out of the narrow windows they could see below them the blue, glistening sea and hear it beating on the beach. Seagulls flew screaming round the tower, and the children fed them with scraps left over from the food they had themselves. At night they sat under the electric light and played games or talked, while above them the great beam played over the surrounding country.

Towards the side from which they had come neither of them ever looked. There were windows all round the tower, but neither Mark nor Marianne ever looked back to the winding road, the plains of long grass, or the empty house with the fence round it.

Every day Mark climbed the steps six times: there were a hundred steps, he told Marianne. 'Far more than I drew,' she said. His right leg was now no weaker than the left: and Marianne was amazed to see him arrive at the top of the tower, after running up the steps, hardly breathing faster than normal. He ate enormously whatever Marianne could think of to draw for him, and visibly put on weight. Marianne, who was now able to move round her own house at home, and copy from life, drew as good a picture as she could of their bathroom weighing machine and on this, in the tower, they charted Mark's amazing gains.

'I wonder if you're putting on weight in real life,' Marianne said, when he had reached the great total of eight and a half stone. 'I wish you could remember. Haven't you any idea what's happening to you?'

'No,' Mark said positively. 'I haven't much. I have a sort of feeling it's all right there. You know. Quite different from at first when you came to the house. I think I knew then that something was wrong, but I still don't know what.'

'I know,' Marianne said. 'I'll ask Miss Chesterfield. She knows what's going on in your home and she'll tell me.'

So the ridiculous situation arose that Marianne was able to tell Mark that Miss Chesterfield reported that he, Mark, was out of bed, doing mild exercises, walking almost without a limp, with every prospect of leading an absolutely normal life in a matter of months. 'She says your breathing is perfectly all right,' Marianne said. 'And you'll never have to use that respirator apparatus again. I asked her if you could run upstairs, and she said, no, not yet, and of course you can't bicycle there or do half the things you do here.'

'It's funny, isn't it?' Mark said thoughtfully. 'How much further on I am here than there? I wonder how much I weigh there?'

'I can't ask that,' Marianne answered. 'Miss Chesterfield would think it was extraordinary, and I couldn't possibly explain.'

The summer was coming to an end when Marianne went out for her first walk. The leaves which had been so new and green when she had gone to bed, were dusty now and hung liked tired banners on the trees. The town was hot and the air smelt used-up and exhausted. People complained of the drought and the heat, and Marianne's mother was surprised to see how little it affected her convalescent daughter: she had no idea that at night Marianne walked on the cliffs and drew in lungfuls of fresh salt wind from the restless dancing sea.

'I've filled my drawing book,' Marianne said triumphantly to Mark one night as they sat in the upper tower room. 'I've drawn so much to put in here, that I haven't got room for a single thing more.'

'You've filled the tower, too,' Mark said, looking round the room, which certainly had a cluttered look. 'If you put in any more we shan't be able to get up and downstairs. I've had to put the last lot of books on the steps as it is, since you drew in that model railway all round the walls. You know we really didn't need that.'

'No, but it's fun,' Marianne said, unrepentantly. 'I saw one in a house we went to tea at the day before yesterday, and I thought you'd like to play with it.'

'I do. It's a smashing one. But don't draw any more, or we honestly shan't have room to move.'

'All right. Or I'll only draw little teeny things that won't get in our way, like chewing-gum or pencils or india-rubbers.'

'Marianne!' said Mark suddenly, after a brief pause.

'Yes, what?'

'Have you thought at all how we're going to get out of here?'

'No. Why should we get out? We're all right here, aren't we?'

'No!' Mark said. 'I'm not. I don't want to stop up here for ever. It's not dangerous like the house was, I know that, but there isn't enough room.'

'I know the rooms are a bit crowded,' Marianne admitted, looking round. 'But we don't have to stay in here in the daytime. We can always go out on the cliff.'

'Yes, I know. But we've done that so often. I want something different now.'

'Where do you want to go?' Marianne asked, irritated and hurt by his not finding her tower and her cliffs good enough.

'I want to get down to the sea.'

Directly he had said it, Marianne recognized with the most inside part of her that he had said what she wanted too. Suddenly the tower became to her too only a resting place, a place to stop at and go on from, not the final refuge it had seemed before.

'Yes,' she said, 'I hadn't thought of that. I think I do, too. But how can we? The cliffs are much too steep to climb down. Perhaps I could draw a ladder?'

'My good girl, you couldn't possibly draw a ladder long enough to reach a quarter of the height we are above the sea. And if you did, we couldn't manage to let it down from here. It'd be much too big to handle.'

'A rope ladder?' Marianne suggested.

'I don't fancy climbing down a rope ladder that isn't fastened at the bottom, for about 500 feet, myself,' Mark said coldly.

'Perhaps if we walked far enough along the cliffs we'd find a way down,' Marianne said.

'I don't see any sign of it, do you? All along as far as you can see it's just these enormous great cliffs without any way down. And we've walked quite a distance both ways and never seen a sign of a possible way to the beach.'

'Well, you suggest something then,' Marianne said crossly.

'A helicopter,' Mark said promptly. It was obvious that he had thought about the problem and had the answer ready.

'A helicopter! Oh, yes, that'd be marvellous. But do you know how to fly one?'

'Oh, no. There'd have to be a pilot in it already. But I thought it'd be like this lighthouse. You drew it as a lighthouse, and there was someone to make the light work. We didn't have to bother about that.'

[167]

The children, though they could get out on to the battlements round the glass dome which enclosed the light, had never penetrated into the dome itself, and had not discovered how the beam was thrown, or what or who set the mechanism working at night.

'Ye-es,' Marianne said. 'I suppose that would be all right. If I drew it up in the air already it would have to have a pilot, wouldn't it? But, Mark, I don't think I could draw a helicopter. I don't know what it looks like properly.'

'I could,' Mark said promptly.

Marianne stared at him.

'But I've got the pencil!' she exclaimed.

'You could let me have it for that.'

'But it's mine! I mean, what I draw with it comes true here. You came because I drew you. If I gave you the pencil perhaps I wouldn't be here myself.'

'Well, if I am when you draw, why shouldn't you be when I draw?'

'It wouldn't be the same. I wouldn't know whether I was going to be here or not, if I couldn't draw something to make sure of coming.'

'Well?' said Mark. 'I've never known.'

'It might not work if you did the drawing even if I did give you the pencil,' Marianne argued.

'Well, are you prepared to try?'

There was a pause.

'I think I could draw a helicopter myself,' Marianne said. Mark looked at her.

'I expect I could find a picture in one of Thomas's books and copy it.'

'Well, don't make a mess of it,' Mark said, with a sigh. 'We don't want some infernal machine hovering over us and dropping bombs on us or something, just because you can't draw a helicopter and are too beastly bossy to let me have any say in what goes on round here.'

These words were still ringing in Marianne's ears in her

real-life day following the dream. To make sure that she did not incur the risk Mark had spoken of, she practised drawing helicopters with an ordinary pencil, not The Pencil. Thomas's books had not yielded anything she could copy: and her attempts at drawing an aeroplane with a fly-wheel spinning on top – Thomas's description of his idea of a helicopter – looked more like enormous angry insects or indeed infernal machines, as Mark had suggested. Marianne did not want any of the objects she had drawn hovering over the tower.

'You look tired,' said her mother, coming into the sitting-room where Marianne was resting. 'It is terribly hot and muggy today, even in here and this is the coolest room in the house.'

'I'm all right!' Marianne said wearily. She pushed her drawing book and pencils away from her and, leaning her head against a cushion, shut her eyes.

'Poor girl,' her mother said. 'You are a limp rag in this heat. Never mind, I've got good news for you. Dr. Burton says you're well enough to go away now, so I'm going to take you out of this stuffy town to get some fresh air.'

'Where?' said Marianne, only half listening.

'To the sea.'

'The sea!' Marianne sat upright, awake instantly. 'Where? When? How soon can we go?'

'Next week,' her mother said, smiling to see Marianne's excitement. 'I couldn't get the rooms any sooner or I'd have liked to take you now, straight away. But if you can hang on for another few days without collapsing, my darling, the sea winds will soon make you feel more lively.'

'So I shall get to the sea,' Marianne thought, 'even if I can't draw a helicopter. I don't need to bother about trying any more. I expect Mark's mother and father will take him to the sea to recover, too.'

'It's *my* pencil,' she thought. 'I found it. It was in my great-grandmother's workbox. I've done everything with it.

[169]

I've got all sorts of things specially for Mark with it that I didn't want myself. I haven't been selfish.'

'Lots of times I've drawn things he suggested,' she thought. 'I haven't always done just what I wanted and not what he did. And anyway I've managed very well. I got Mark out of that house, and I got us both up the hills to the tower. He couldn't possibly have done that by himself. I had to be bossy then, as he calls it, or we'd never have reached the top. I don't see why I should let him arrange everything now, and perhaps make things different from how I'd like them.'

She tried again to draw a helicopter, but rubbed it out impatiently.

'Anyway, if I did want to give him the pencil I don't know how to do it. I couldn't ask Miss Chesterfield to take it, she wouldn't understand: and, anyhow, the real Mark she knows mayn't remember the dream and wouldn't know what it was for. I can't do it, even if I wanted to, so I'll tell Mark that. He'll have to think of some other way of getting out. I'll just put in the chewing-gum to make sure I get back there tonight.'

She took up the pencil and drew a small packet of chewing-gum in the very small space remaining to her. She remembered that she had said she would draw something else.

'I said pencils,' she thought. 'I will. I'll draw pencils. Ordinary pencils, not this pencil.'

But one pencil is very like another. It is difficult, when you are drawing an ordinary lead pencil, not very long, and nicely sharpened, to make it look very different from any other, not so ordinary pencil, also not very long and nicely sharpened. The pencil Marianne drew in the upper room in the tower was indistinguishable from the pencil she held in her hand. It was The Pencil.

'I'll rub it out,' Marianne thought, and remembered immediately that The Pencil could not be rubbed out.

[170]

'I'll think of it as an ordinary pencil, and then it will be,' she thought. 'After all the pack of cards had the right number of cards in it because I thought it.'

She looked at her drawing sternly, and tried to think the pencil ordinary. But it wouldn't do. She knew, she had known as soon as she had drawn it, that it was her own pencil she had put in the tower room, and that whether she liked it or not, she had got to let Mark have it. The pencil had done its last piece of magic for her; it had as it were, deliberately drawn itself, and so said good-bye.

Marianne sighed.

'Perhaps it is his turn to have it,' she said, and sighed again.

That night she put the pencil in a prominent place on her bedside table.

'I wonder if you'll be here tomorrow morning,' she thought sadly.

In the tower – it was daylight there – something had changed. Marianne could not make up her mind whether it was her imagination that made her feel an alteration in the atmosphere, or whether it was fact. Mark was preoccupied and rather cross; it appeared that he did not want to talk. They went out and walked along the short springy turf that crowned the cliffs: the seagulls screamed above them, and the sea, very blue and green and white, crisped on the stones far below on the beach: but Mark did not talk much and answered Marianne only by 'yes' or 'no'.

'What's the matter?' Marianne was at last provoked into saying. 'Are you feeling ill, Mark? Or are you cross with me about something?'

'I'm thinking,' Mark said. 'That's all.'

'Oh!'

After a pause, Mark said, with difficulty, 'It isn't my being cross with you. The thing is, aren't you cross with me?'

'What for?' Marianne asked in surprise.

'I was beastly last time. About your pencil. Of course you

[171]

keep it. It's yours, and I didn't mean that I wanted to have it as a present, you know. I only thought perhaps I could borrow it so as to get us out.'

'It's quite all right, Mark. Please don't –'

'No, it isn't. I've been feeling beastly ever since. I shouldn't have said that.'

'What?'

'About your being bossy. You've been jolly kind and I shan't ever forget how you wouldn't go without me, out of the house and up the road, when THEY might have got you because of me. I wanted to say, I'm sorry. There!'

For a moment Marianne couldn't say anything. Then she said, 'It's jolly nice of you to say so, and it's quite all right. I haven't been thinking about it at all. Anyway, you're quite right, I was being bossy.'

'Don't,' Mark said.

'I must. Because I wanted to tell you that I've brought it with me. There. It's for you.'

She held out her hand. When she had woken into the dream she had found the pencil in her hand, and she had kept it there ever since.

'What is it?' Mark said, in surprise.

'The pencil.'

'That? It looks just like an ordinary one.'

'It isn't,' Marianne said, a little hurt. 'It's The Pencil. I know it doesn't look very special, but it's awfully nice to draw with.'

'Yes, it does look as if it would write well,' Mark said quickly. 'But I can't take it. What would you do if I couldn't get it back to you?'

'I don't want it,' Marianne said. 'I want you to have it. You're quite right, Mark. I can't draw a helicopter so that it looks like anything. You draw one and then we'll be able to get away.'

'I don't know what to draw on,' Mark said, hesitating.

'We've got lots of paper in the tower: don't you remember

[172]

there's a drawing block we used for playing Consequences? Come on! Draw it now.'

They went back into the tower. Marianne found the drawing block, but Mark still held back.

'Come on,' she urged.

'But if I take your pencil, perhaps you won't be able to get back here.'

'I don't want to get back. I want to get out, like you.'

'Yes, I know, but you've got to get back here so that you can get out. I mean, if you just stay away in what you call real life, you'll never know whether you're really not still here. Not free. See what I mean?'

'Yes. But in my real life I am free, and I'm going to the sea,' Marianne said.

'I still think this counts, too,' Mark said. 'I think you ought to be able to get to this sea as well as the other one. Anyway I want to.'

'I tell you what,' Marianne said. 'You draw me in the tower. After all, you were in the house when I drew you, so I'll be here if you draw me. Then you can put in a helicopter and we'll both get out.'

'All right. If you're quite sure about letting me have the pencil.'

'I'm quite sure.'

'It's jolly decent of you,' Mark said. He took the pencil and sat looking at the blank sheet of the drawing block.

'Go on, draw,' said Marianne impatiently.

'I can't with you looking,' Mark said. 'It's too embarrassing. I don't want to be rude, but couldn't you go out, or something, while I'm doing it?'

'All right,' said Marianne, and went.

She lay down on the top of the cliff and looked out to sea. It was as real as any sea she had ever seen, full of changing colours and laced with little white waves racing across the surface. The lisp of the water on the stones below and the tinkle of the stones falling back into place as the waves receded was just as Marianne remembered the sea of her other life. Only this scene was uninhabited, except for herself and Mark. No bathers ever shouted on the beach, no ships ever crossed the expanse of water or broke the perfect curve where sea met sky.

Marianne lay and looked at the sea and the sky, which was bright and decorated with little flounces of cloud, until her eyes ached. She closed them and slept on the top of the cliff in her dream.

19. The Empty Tower

Preparations for going away went on enthusiastically all round Marianne: she was even considered well enough to help in some of them. She had grown so much longer with being in bed, that she had to have an almost completely new outfit of clothes, which was amusing. She helped her mother pack luggage, and tidy the house, take down curtains for cleaning and sort out the winter clothes they would need when they came back. It was delightful to find that she could do all these things without being tired: that the more she did, in fact, the more energetic she felt. Dr Burton had given her permission to do anything she felt like and had stopped visiting the house. 'You can run, you can swim, you can play leap-frog or cricket or do anything within reason,' he said. 'Don't go and try a two-mile marathon, or let yourself get absolutely tired out. You've done very well, and I'm very much pleased with you. Now go away and forget that you ever had this illness and had to be careful and stay in bed. Just do whatever you feel you can and you'll be all right.'

So the days passed, actively and agreeably. But for some reason or other, at night Marianne did not dream. At first she had hardly noticed, she was too much occupied with other things: but when she had time to remember, she wondered what was happening in the tower by the sea and why she had not found herself there before. She had no means now of getting herself back: the pencil had gone, as she had known it would. She searched half-heartedly in her pencil-box and even looked again in the workbox in which she had first found it. But it had disappeared and Marianne felt it was for good.

Miss Chesterfield was also leaving. She was going to Dartmoor where, she told Marianne, her parents had a grey stone house on the moors, just above a little river which ran shallowly over brown stones and was full of lazy spotted trout. Wild ponies came often to the garden walls, and there were tors to climb and moors all round, where you might walk for a day and never meet another soul.

'It sounds lovely,' Marianne said, when Miss Chesterfield described it to her on their last morning of lessons. 'But I'd rather go to the sea.'

'That's what Mark says,' Miss Chesterfield said, packing her books away in her case for the last time.

'Mark? Why? Is he going to the sea, too?'

'Yes. In a day or two. He's so much better than the doctors ever thought he could be in such a short time, that he's going away tomorrow or the next day – I can't remember which – and they think he'll be able to do everything quite normally. Especially swim, of course. That will do more than anything to get his legs absolutely strong again.'

'Where's he going?'

'Down to Cornwall, I think, or it may be Devon. His mother did tell me, but I'm afraid I've forgotten. It's somewhere where there's a warm salt-water swimming bath I know, so that Mark can bathe even if it's too cold to swim in the sea.'

'Oh,' said Marianne. 'It would be funny if we'd been going to the same place, wouldn't it? When we've both been ill at the same time and both had you to teach us and all that.'

'Yes, it would,' Miss Chesterfield said, and there the subject dropped. Miss Chesterfield said good-bye, and gave Marianne, as a parting present, a book. (It was Rolf Boldrewood's *Robbery Under Arms*, and Marianne found it wildly exciting.) Marianne, in her turn, gave Miss Chesterfield a small cushion with a bright cover made of patchwork, which she had been working at hard for the last few weeks.

'It's lovely, Marianne,' said Miss Chesterfield warmly. 'Thank you very much indeed. I shall keep it on the chair I generally sit in and think of you whenever it supports my exhausted head.'

'And thank you for the book,' Marianne said, 'it looks marvellous. All about horses and bushrangers and people shooting each other. Thanks frightfully, it's terribly good of you.'

Altogether the farewell took place in a friendly and generous atmosphere. And the next day Marianne and her family were to go to the sea.

That night, at last, she dreamed.

She stood outside the tower, just as weeks, months, years ago, she had stood outside the house. Everything was as usual – the wind-flecked sky, the bright, glittering sea, the dark land behind. The seagulls floated and swung above her, and the sun was warm on her back and arms as she went up to the tower, swung the door open, and went in.

It was cool and dark inside the lower room compared to the sparkle outside. Marianne climbed to the upper room in search of Mark, and then on up to the battlements, but in vain. He was not there.

'He must be somewhere outside,' she thought, and she went out again into the sunshine and walked round the tower and called again. But no one replied. Mark had gone.

'He's left me all alone,' Marianne thought, half-frightened and very angry. 'Directly I gave him my pencil he went and got himself out of this place and left me behind. I didn't leave him behind when he couldn't walk properly, but he's gone off in his beastly helicopter and left me without any way of getting out. He hasn't even left me the pencil.'

She said this without at all knowing whether he had or not: now she went over to the table to make sure. There, placed so that she should see it directly she turned her eyes towards it, was the drawing block. On the top sheet was a neat, workmanlike drawing of the tower; every window was placed with mathematical precision, every battlement proportioned right. Outside it, on the top of the cliff stood a little figure which Marianne recognized for herself. Up in the air hovered a small but very efficient-looking helicopter with a rope ladder dangling from it.

At the bottom of the page were some lines of writing.

The helicopter has been hovering around all day. I don't want to go till you come, but as they seem to be waiting for me, I think perhaps I'd better. Don't worry – I will make them come back and fetch you as soon as I can. Won't it be terrific to get to the sea at last? Thanks awfully for the pencil, it seems to have done the trick.

Mark.

The pencil was nowhere to be seen.

Marianne put down the picture, and relief flooded her. He had not deserted her, he had waited for her, he had not wanted to go without her, he would come back and fetch her. The tower was no longer lonely or unfriendly or frightening. Nor was it any longer a place of refuge. It was a place of departure.

She went out again into the sunshine. She could hear the hum of drowsy bees, searching for honey, the wailing cry of the seagulls, and, at the cliff's foot, the lapping of small lacy waves. Here, in the dream, it was a golden afternoon; the sea and the land were at peace with each other; even the dark country behind the hills was wrapped in a soft grey haze which was gentle, not frightening, at one with the beauty of the day.

Everything seemed to be resting; content; waiting.

Mark would come: he would take her to the sea. Marianne lay down on the short, sweet-smelling turf. She would wait, too.

FABER CHILDREN'S CLASSICS

The Children of Green Knowe
by Lucy Boston

The River at Green Knowe
by Lucy Boston

The Mouse and His Child
by Russell Hoban

Marianne Dreams
by Catherine Storr

The Mirror Image Ghost
by Catherine Storr

Make Lemonade
by Virginia Euwer Wolff